deadly

deadly

JULIE CHIBBARO

ILLUSTRATIONS BY JEAN-MARC SUPERVILLE SOVAK

SCHOLASTIC INC.
New York Toronto London Auckland
Sydney Mexico City New Delhi Hong Kong

ISBN 978-0-545-40412-9

Text copyright © 2011 by Julie Chibbaro.
Illustrations copyright © 2011 by Jean-Marc Superville Sovak. All rights reserved.
Published by Scholastic Inc., 557 Broadway, New York, NY 10012, by arrangement with Atheneum Books for Young Readers, an imprint of Simon & Schuster Children's Publishing Division. SCHOLASTIC and associated logos are trademarks and/or registered trademarks of Scholastic Inc.

12 11 10 9 8 7 6 5 4 3   12 13 14 15 16/0

Printed in the U.S.A.   40

First Scholastic printing, October 2011

Book design by Sonia Chaghatzbanian
The text for this book is set in Goudy Old Style.
The illustrations for this book are rendered in ink.
Illustration of Mary Mallon on page 247 is from the *New York American*, June 20, 1909.

For Samsa and Audrey

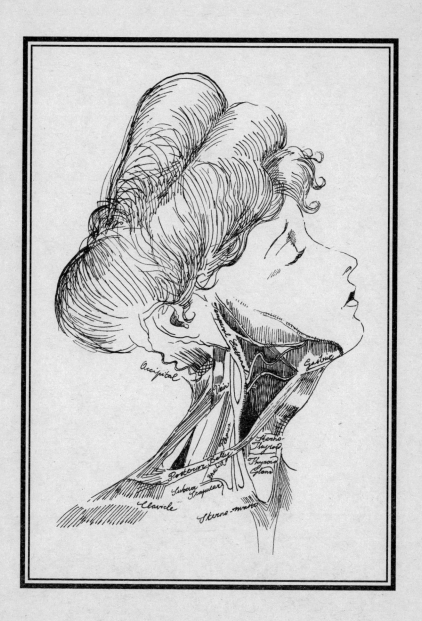

September 7, 1906

I know that one day I won't be on this earth anymore. A world without the physical me—what will that look like? I'll seep down into the soil, become a plant, a tree; I'll be falling leaves, yellow, crunching under a child's feet until I am dust. Nothing. Gone.

Every September, the shivers come over me, thoughts of my brother's terrifying death, and the questions—why did his short life end? Why do people have to die?

I write here, trying to explain, each word a stepping stone. These words illuminate my past; they bring me forward, to the future. They help me remember.

Without my writing, I would suffer an emptiness worse than I feel now.

Today there are great holes in me. I feel like a secret observer, separate from everything that goes on around me.

Peering from my window just above the storefronts of this creaky building on Ludlow Street where I've lived since the morning of my birth, I watch Mrs. Zanberger at the vegetable cart below. She argues with Miss Lara over the price of onions the way she does every Sunday. Behind her, Kat Radlikov drags her heavy skirt through the mud, her belly swollen, her husband hiding in the shadows of their rooms. In front of the grocer's, Ruth Schmidt smiles under her patched parasol at Izzy Moscowitz, who works too hard to notice her. I see the Feldman sisters from upstairs chasing each other through puddles like boys, with finally a morning free from the factory. Under the butcher's canopy, their mother talks with other mothers from the neighborhood, their faces dark with worry.

I know them, these girls and women, I've seen their families grow, they've seen mine get smaller. When I'm in their company, I listen to them trade recipes and sewing tips, I smile at their gossip about each other, yet I can't find a word to add. My eyes get stuck on the sadness in their mouths, or their red, chapped hands, and suddenly I'm imagining their lives—what they dream about when no one is looking, or what they might be like with fewer children. The women talk around and over me; somehow I feel like I'll always be looking at them through a distant window.

Even at school, I feel this. When classes started this week, I had in my mind the birth I'd attended with Marm the night before—Sophie Gersh came due around midnight and her mother pounded at our door, her fear thrusting us from our beds. Marm and I rushed after the frightened woman, running full gallop the two blocks to her daughter's apartment, where the girl's husband stood outside wringing his hands, and she lay keening in the bedroom like a poor abandoned child. I took my place at the head of the bed, where I held Sophie's hand and wiped the sweat from her teary eyes and assured her the birth would be good, that all would come out as we planned. Below, Marm did her magic; Sophie's water broke, she was ready. Working together, the three of us encouraged her baby to come forth into this world. His birth happened easily, a miracle, one of those rare times when Marm and I can clean up the infant and hand him to his mother and happily return to our own beds. We napped an hour before rising to face the day, which was my first day of school.

My schoolmates kissed—we don't see each other through the summer months; the girls had matured, their faces and bodies grown longer or fatter. I smiled at Josephine, who had become impossibly taller and thinner and prettier, and Fanny, whose round face had finally found its cheekbones. I brushed their cheeks with my lips. I searched their eyes for the start to a conversation; I wanted to tell them about the birth, or Benny, but Josephine started talking about her new job at the perfume counter at Macy's. She described the glamorous ladies who bought the most expensive ounces, the delicate fabrics they wore, their jewels and dogs. She didn't stop until Mrs. Browning came in with stout Miss Ruben, our teacher for the year. My heart dropped when I saw it was her. Miss Ruben's eyes swept the room imperiously and settled on me.

She said, "Girls, I see that some of you are still lacking in the most basic charms. We must correct that situation now. This is your last year before you are released into the world. There is no time left to waste!"

I turned my eyes away from hers and concentrated on the smoke I could see puffing from the stack of the building next door. My stomach soured at the thought of spending my last year with her. Miss Ruben hasn't liked me since third grade.

At afternoon lunch, I sat in the common room nibbling on my potato knish, listening to Jo and Fanny, feeling as if my insides were made of India rubber and all their words bounced around without touching me. I again attempted to tell them about the beautiful boy whose birth I had witnessed that very morning, but Josephine's exuberant chatter drowned out my words before I could form them.

"Oh, Fanny," she said, "goodness, I forgot to tell you I thought you looked simply darling at the cocoon tea! Where did you buy that sweet dress?"

"Feinstein's had a special sale," Fanny explained. "I saw Dora there, and she convinced me to buy it. Did you hear her father caught her and Mr. Goldwaite holding hands in the back of his carriage? That man is too old for her!"

"He should pair with a dumpling like Miss Ruben, not a girl Dora's age!" Josephine said. "Have you noticed the way our teacher looks this year? That lip coloring is simply awful on her, don't you think? And doesn't she know gray jackets with heavy braids are out of fashion?"

"The way she looks at us," Fanny said, "you'd think she was the Queen of England!"

The girls laughed, and I shook my head. I longed to be somewhere else, with someone else. I felt inside me that sore place of missing Anushka, and that silly flash of anger—why has she left me alone? Every morning we'd walk to school together, talking about everything under the sun. She'd ask me what I dreamt and thought about. No one does that now. I wish she hadn't moved away last spring. In her letters from the farm, she writes about someone named Ida. I get a pang of fear when she writes of this girl. I hope Ida has not replaced me. Anushka said speaking to Ida was profound, like walking into a lake and suddenly discovering a drop-off into deeper water.

Oh, I simply ache to have a profound talk with another girl! I'd tell her about Papa and Benny, how our life used to be.

I've been sneaking into the temple to read notices on the B'nai community board, those that are not in Hebrew. For our last year of school, we are allowed to work afternoons, but I can't imagine myself arranging flowers like Sara does at McLean's Fancy Florist, or using my feminine charms like Josephine to draw in customers at Macy's perfumery. Mrs. Browning says these sorts of jobs bring us closer to the class of people we strive to be someday, but I want serious employ. Not just for the money, though Marm and I do need it, but for the challenge to my mind. I want to be able to go somewhere and do something important and return home in the evening with soft bills in hand. Is it foolish to want a different type of job than Mrs. Browning trains us for, something more, something bigger than myself?

Truthfully, I hunger for a job that's meaningful.

September 9, 1906

Can a girl get work fighting death? I feel strange writing that—but it's the question that always comes to me, even in my dreams. I've seen so much death. I find it's better not to talk about it, to push those pictures out of my mind. But in here, with the alchemy of pen to paper, something happens to me, and these terrible thoughts emerge full-blown. Here, I can confess that I see sickness like a violent weed growing everywhere, in the rubbish bins that puff out ash clouds, in the dirty puddles that ooze in the streets, in the breath of the gin ladies who hang about the sidewalk, in the dead cats, the hungry mice that gnaw at the walls, when I go walking in the park and see packs of stray dogs making garbage of the city.

I see death whenever I pass a brown horse.

What are these entities that weaken us and make us

die? How is it that death is here on earth? How does it enter people's bodies and sicken them, kill them?

If we knew how to fight death, could we have saved Benny's life?

I can't help thinking of my big brother at this time, the start of the new school term. He was nearly the same age I am now, a high school boy. We were walking home from temple when that brown horse came from nowhere and trampled right over him, that man charging down the street in such a hurry, he didn't stop, he never stopped to see what he had done to Benny. I can still feel the wind of the horse, its closeness to my face as it sped by. We were talking together, none of us saw it. Marm cried out and Papa scooped Benny up and ran home with him.

I'll never forget the terror on Marm's face when she brought Dr. Barnes, and Benny's cries when the doctor straightened his leg bones and bandaged the bloodied skin. In the next weeks, the unhealed sores turned green and spread over my brother's battered legs. How useless were Dr. Barnes's visits, with his Blood Cure and his Cooling Glass and his Silver Mend. He couldn't make those sores go away.

Benny got so much worse, and Papa stayed with him, never left his side. He sat with him all day long, feeding him and washing up after him. He changed his bandages, releasing the sour, infected smell of poor Benny's wounds. Every night in this front room, I slept beside my brother. I curled my head into his back and listened to his low moans until that final night, when the sounds ended.

I'll always think there was some way we could've helped him, if only we knew how.

September 11, 1906

I spend my free nights assisting Marm, delivering life, watching young mothers struggle, and I feel somehow that I'm not really helping, that I don't understand how to lessen the pain these new mothers endure. The Radlikov birthing last night was particularly hard on poor Kat, who pushed and moaned from that place of isolation where all birth-giving women seem to go. I spread warm cloths over her forehead and rubbed her from shoulder to waist and squeezed her hands as if I could squeeze out the child myself. Marm positioned her properly and told her happy stories of good births. For hours she cried and rested and cried until, at last, a boy came out. But the afterbirth didn't follow; instead, the waves continued. Marm boiled water and cleaned her tools. I tried my best to soothe Kat by pressing warm towels into her lower back.

Marm felt the girl's belly; she helped Kat push again. Out came a second little surprise! We all gasped when we saw that inside poor Kat were two tiny boys each no bigger than my shoe! It was my first twin birth—I never imagined what it might look like, a woman borning two separate creatures the way animals litter two, three, and four. We laughed and wept with Kat, we bathed the newborns for her and her husband, and we went home.

I spent the day in school exhausted.

I feel, when I am holding a birthing woman for hours on end, like I'm trying to physically absorb her pain with my own body, to take her burden from her through my hands and mind so it won't hurt so much, so she won't scream and cry, so she will just think of the baby who is coming. Afterwards, if all went well, I feel empty, tired deep down in my bones.

September 12, 1906

The army check came; it always comes just as we begin to reach into the kettle where we keep our rainy-day pennies. Even though we've been receiving the check every month for years now, it stirs up feelings for us, especially for Marm, ones she can't talk about, and she sends me to cash it at the grocer's as quickly as I can. I put the stub with the others inside the beautiful book Papa gave me just before he left for war. That book is the most precious thing I own. I hope one day I can understand even a few of all these mysterious subjects:

Year Book of Facts in Science and Arts, for 1897, Exhibiting the Most Important Improvements in Mechanics, Useful and Natural Philosophy, Chemistry,

Astronomy, Zoology, Botany, Mineralogy,
Meteorology, and Geology, Along with
Obituaries of Eminent Scientific Men

The brown ink of the inscription has faded, his only writing to me that I have:

Darling Prudent One—
May this book make the world
more transparent to you.
Your papa, 1898

I study his elegant penmanship, and wonder how he learned it, since he was a machinist in Nolan's Ball Bearing Factory, and before that a newsie on the street. I must ask him about his interest in scientific matters when he returns, for I don't know how it began, and Marm won't say, even though she gave me my first tablet and got me started on drawing and writing, copying from Papa's book.

I remember watching the clock, seeing the moment it went from 1899 to 1900, the thrill of that instant, that shift in time. All the bells in town rang; our neighbors banged on the walls and filled the streets with noisemakers and hollered about the new century. Marm handed me that tablet, the one with the red silk cover. She said, Prudence, you need to start keeping a record. You must write events like these down. Time passes in a steady march, nothing ever gets in its way, and you must remember things.

I knew she meant that I must write for Papa. And I did that, for years.

I don't know when I stopped writing for him, and started simply writing.

Remember. I must remember him. He has dark, curly hair, and his features are small and sharp in his perfectly oval face. He is taller than Marm by a few inches, but not as tall as Benny. He's a serious man, but he laughs with his whole face. His hands smell of metal and gefilte fish, which he makes sometimes himself in the meat grinder. He calls me Oh Prudent One, and says he named me for the sensible look on my face when I was born.

I wonder, every day I wonder, where I could write him a letter. Missing in the Field—how can one address a letter to a person who is missing?

Better not to wonder such things at all.

Marm always tells me how my father's father fought in the Civil War for his adopted Northern city; he cut off his long black beard and died somewhere in the South a hero, defending a hill. I don't know if he ever told anyone he was a Jewish soldier; I imagine he couldn't yet speak English. Marm has never had patience for the religious; when we sat shivah for Benny after he died, she didn't accept Mrs. Zanberger's gifts of food or Rabbi Samsfield's spiritual help. Papa wanted to continue the prayers, I think, but she asked our neighbors to leave and ended the shivah two days early, which began an argument with my father, who went to the Spanish War shortly after, and has not returned.

I still hear bits of words from the arguments Papa and Marm had after Benny's death, words like "gone" or "God" or "go," though I can't remember whole sentences, or meanings. I have to wonder if their arguing was what caused him to leave us.

I think Marm couldn't endure her thoughts about Benny anymore and my father didn't understand that. Every day, until I was eight years old, Benny and Papa sat with us here in this very room where I sit. Benny's long legs and arms took up the space beside our stove, the way he settled himself, all angles, nearly a man. Under the window I slept beside him, his head at my feet, which he would tickle to wake me in the morning before he went off to work with Papa in the factory.

At night they brought us fresh rye bread and chopped chicken livers to eat and served them when Marm was too tired to cook. Their laughter filled our lives, and now they are both gone. A quiet has grown over us like a heavy fungus, every year another inch of thick white matter, covering us.

Neither Marm nor I can bear to speak of them.

She wrote so many letters to the government looking for my father after the war ended. Their return notice claimed soldier 3040, Gregory Galewski, Missing in the Field. His body has not been found, they said. He will come home someday; I store in my heart that hope. I am grateful the government began to send us my father's pay after they declared him missing; they send pay to Mrs. Finkel's family too. We all so very much need the money. I must get a job, and soon.

September 14, 1906

Marm suggested I go to the employment agencies to look for work, as well as checking the boards and the newspapers. I sent letters to six job advertisements in the *American*, and two from the board, but no one has made any offerings. I feel it has nothing to do with my skills, as I can type faster than any girl in our class, and I've told no one that I'm Jewish, so I'm not sure what I'm doing wrong. I know I shouldn't despair, but I can't help hearing that little squeak of fear that nothing will ever change, that I'll be at Mrs. Browning's School for Girls for the rest of my days, learning to draw portraits and tally numbers in French and paint with watercolors and fashion a proper skirt.

Tonight, as I was preparing for bed, I took down my hair and began to do my hundred strokes when I noticed a long gray growing from my temple, the length of the rest of my hair. Resisting the urge to pluck it from my head, I stretched it between my hands and examined it. Its color is the opposite of the rest of my hair, a stark white in the raven blackness, its quality so different, like wire nestled in a bed of silk threads. How is it that a sixteen-year-old girl is growing gray, and what causes the hair to change color so abruptly? Maybe I'm becoming someone else, and will wake with a whole head of grays one morning, and a new name. I'll be like Dorian in that Oscar Wilde story, only the opposite will happen to me; I'll become old before my time.

When I consider my hair or nails, these things I can see growing on myself, I wonder why cells take certain shapes. Marm brought home a special edition of the *Scientific American* where a man named Dr. Golgi explained his experiments with cells and the nervous system. The magazine described a cell as a structural unit of living matter, with walls and a little nucleus inside—and I must say, I can't quite see it. I can't see it as a thing alive, not flat as in a drawing. What does it look like, exactly? How is it these cells make up a face, or a body, and not some other form? The very idea of cells, that it takes many hundreds of them to make us, intrigues me. If they are many, and separate, how, then, are we held together? Is it simply gravity, or is there some sort of glue?

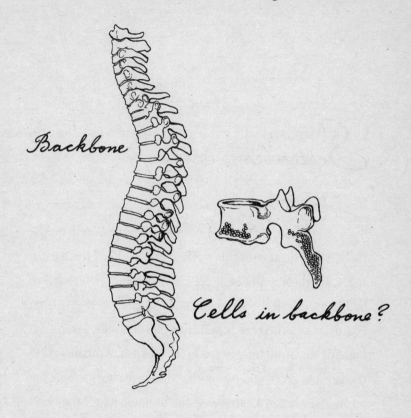

Backbone

Cells in backbone?

Perhaps it's the bones that hold the cells together somehow? But the article said even bones are made of cells—leaving me utterly perplexed. The article did not provide enough answers, and not knowing makes me fear that I may burst into a constellation of infinite points at any moment.

I wish we could afford to buy the *Scientific American* more often; that is another reason to have my own money.

September 16, 1906

Old Mrs. Zanberger fell in the hallway in a dead faint this week. Her mass filled the narrow space, all those years of sweet challah bread, potato latkes, and rugelach, all the stews she makes for her ever-changing boarders, and the breads and fruit pies she sells, layers of it building up, stretching her skin. It took Mr. Zanberger, and the latest boarder, and two of the Moskowitz boys to pick her up and take her in a carriage to the hospital, where they kept her. Marm made her an apple basket and told me to bring it to her. She was in the heart ward with a dozen other women, six beds to either side of the long room, and hers at the end. She was sitting up, trying to embroider. I looked at her closely, the dusty circles that dragged at her puffy eyes, her lips white and fingers swollen, the chins that lay on her chest. I had the chilling feeling I could see her dying one cell at a time.

"When are you getting married?"

She interrupted my examination of her with the question.

I stammered out an answer. "I'm very busy with school."

"You're going to end up like your mother, never able to meet a nice Jewish man because she doesn't go to services. She'll spend the rest of her days lonely if she isn't careful."

I reminded Mrs. Zanberger that we are awaiting my father's return.

She gave me her knowing look and said, "The Jewish New Year, Rosh Hashanah, is coming. I told your mother about the High Holy Day services. You'll be there, yes?" I knew Marm had excused us, as usual, but Mrs. Zanberger didn't wish to take no for an answer.

I shrugged and nodded and shook my head.

Her little eyes found mine, and she said, "Jews are a happy people. Come to service, sing with us, it'll make you smile. You're too serious, just like your papa was."

Is. I wanted to correct her: Just like your papa is. But I didn't.

I often see the Jews spilling out of temple, their children singing Hebrew songs and dancing in the streets. But when I see them building their succhas for the holiday, I feel the religion like a name someone else called me, one I knew didn't belong to me.

Or maybe I just don't feel like celebrating.

"You work too hard," Mrs. Zanberger said. She said I shouldn't be assisting my mother in the nights like I do. Gives me black bags under the eyes, and bags make me look ugly, and ugly doesn't bring the boychiks.

Ugly is Mrs. Zanberger's favorite insult.

I raised my chin and said, "I assist Marm because it makes her job a little easier."

She waved her heavy fingers at me. "Your mother's our best midwife. But why are you doing that work? You go to school."

I said, "Senior girls are expected to work—I'm looking to be an afternoon typist, maybe in a doctor's office, or a hospital."

"Typist, well, that's fine," she said approvingly. "I'll see what I can do to help you."

I looked into her little old eyes and felt the power behind them, the way everyone in our neighborhood honors her word, even seeks it out. Despite her fall, Her Majesty the gossip has not lost her touch.

I kissed the air beside her powdery cheek before I left.

It sinks into me, what she says about Jews being a happy people. A secret part of me longs to join them in the streets and dance in the temple and believe in an entity bigger than myself, one who has a reason for taking away my loved ones. I wish I could talk to the long-bearded Rabbi Samsfield and ask him why my brother died, why my father went away, why can't I talk to anyone, why?

Then I see how easily Mrs. Zanberger can make me weak! How she makes me question the things Marm has taught me. The independence, the dignity.

Marm doesn't talk much about her parents, chased from the old country just like Papa's, only that they worked very hard to give up their language and beliefs to become American. That's how Marm wants me to think of myself, as American, and nothing else. Hard work will bring us good things, Marm says, and not prayers and tradition.

Hard work. If only I could find some.

September 19, 1906

The repeating tunes from Mr. Zito the organ grinder and Mr. Victor the hurdy-gurdy player and the clatter of horse hooves on the cobblestones create a noise so great from the street tonight, I can't sleep. I picture myself in a quiet country place, away from crowds of people, on a farm in Virginia like Anushka. I feel so awfully cramped here when I read Anushka's letters about the acres of land and the fresh air. To run barefoot through the fields of daisies and Queen Anne's lace, to smell the fragrance of tomato and dill right from your own kitchen garden! For years, her father had this idea to live close to the earth, to trade in his bookstore for farmland, and he finally

Anethum graveolens L.
(Dill)

did it, moved the whole family south. I have to admire the bravery in that. And from her letters, it seems the move has made Anushka more adventurous, though she was always the braver one of us. She rides her horse to neighboring farms, hauls hay along with her brothers, works the fields with them. She does things girls wouldn't dare do in this city. I'm not so naturally adventurous; I feel nervous about the visit I have planned to her during the winter holiday. Yet I think of the flicker I saw with Marm tonight about Mr. Peary and his men, the way they explored the Arctic, the years it took to get there. A trip to Virginia hardly seems far at all.

It was Treat Night at the Automatic Vaudeville—we took two pennies from the kettle after supper and went on Mr. Moscowitz's recommendation. He said there was a very fine film about the handsome explorer who's been in all the newspapers with his adventure stories. We don't often go to Treat Nights, but Marm and I both wanted to see Mr. Peary.

The place was packed to the rafters with screaming kids eating peanuts out of paper cones and running onstage to pinch the piano player. When the mustachioed explorer came on the screen, all the girls in the audience cheered. Although Mr. Peary didn't succeed in his polar expedition, we all felt he was a hero for trying. They filmed his schooner, which he named after President Roosevelt; Mr. Peary plans to use the same ship for what he hopes will be a successful return to the North Pole next year.

I can almost taste the arctic air, and feel the crunch of snow beneath my feet, the itch to go somewhere. I feel the push inside myself to do something astonishing with my life. If only I could find the bravery, the daring to take such an adventure, despite my being a girl. I think of Anushka down on the farm, and I remember the first day I met her—she had that sort of wildness even then. She always did.

I remember I stood alone in the corner of Mrs. Browning's first-grade room, watching all the other six-year-old girls pairing up to play a delicate game of cat's cradle. I wondered where they all came from and who they belonged to, these girls. I didn't dare approach a single one of them. Anushka strode up to me and opened her mouth in a wide smile, revealing the startling gap of a missing front tooth. She offered me half of her cradle string. I touched my own teeth—I hadn't yet lost any—and asked if it hurt, losing the one. She poked her tongue through the gap; she looked a little mad doing that. I burst into gales of laughter, and she joined me.

I feel that gap now, like a place beside me where she should be.

Two nights ago I attended the St. Xavier annual without Anushka for the first time—I'm not sure why I bothered to go. Was I hoping to meet someone? I watched all the girls dancing with the fellers, Fanny with Arthur Robertson, Josephine with Willem Stryker, all of them waltzing like grown-ups. I sat, my hands curled like two sleeping dogs in my lap. Nobody asked me to dance. I thought of all the annuals I'd attended, sitting together with my smiling Anushka while the boys made a wide circle around us, glancing at us as if we were storefront curiosities, but nothing desirable enough to engage.

This year, I had no one to smile with.

It's like opening a lock, making a new friend; the key must fit exactly right.

September 21, 1906

An opportunity has finally come! I received a note sent from an office expressing interest in me as typist and general note taker. The man set next Tuesday for our meeting time—which seems like years away. Oh, I have thought and hoped so long for this chance, have imagined it so much—walking into an office or hospital in my one good maroon shirtwaist and skirt set, my black hat, my boots polished to a soft sheen. I hope I don't ruin it with my over-enthusiasm or get too flustered to type properly.

When I told Marm that it's a government job with the Department of Health and Sanitation, she held up her hand and disappeared into her room. She keeps private papers and pictures and my father's things in that room; I do not go in there.

After a bit, she returned with an old *Scribner's* maga-zine. "This came out the year before you were born," she said.

"But now I think it'll be interesting for you."

She opened to an article spread with many detailed draw-ings based on photographs of buildings and their insides: dirty children sleeping on wood floors, drunks in alleys, flophouses filled to the brim with raggedy men, boys in pants tied up with rope. I had seen these photographs before in Anushka's father's bookstore, in a famous book called *How the Other Half Lives*.

"Jacob Riis, the journalist," I said.

"This was his first big article," Marm said. "Look closely at that one." She pressed a finger to the page. I bent down, and saw it was our building! Before the improvements, before they tore down the shacks in front and installed the toilets and the running water and the airshaft.

"He came to our tenement and he began writing these reports and taking pictures," Marm said. "The streets of the city were filled with chickens and pigs that would eat the trash people threw out the windows. There were no sweepers back then, nobody paid attention to how dirty our buildings were. Not until Jacob Riis wrote about us."

My mind raced as I stared at the pictures with new eyes—I thought of the job.

Marm said, "I don't even think there was a Department of Health back then." She went to the window and looked out and said, "The streets were horrifying—with horse manure piled as high as ten feet in some places. Ten feet of manure. That's higher than our ceiling."

I stood beside her, looking out.

"It wasn't easy, making changes," Marm said. "Homes had to be demolished, some people disappeared, some were even arrested."

I wonder if things are so different now. Despite the beginning chill of autumn, I can still smell the rubbish in the bins underneath our window; across the street, our fishmonger still throws the innards onto the cobblestones; our neighbors still fall ill with sicknesses they pass to each other, our girls still die in childbirth.

But ten feet of manure, we don't suffer from that. If the city has changed so much in the years since Marm was a girl, how might I help to change it further? It seems a neverending task, keeping after the thousands of people who live in this city, making sure they have clean streets and good health and decent places to live. It seems, finally, just the sort of job I've been looking for, one that is far bigger than me.

Dead horse on Orchard St.
Day 2.

September 25, 1906

I had my interview this morning. I was very nervous, and I'm not sure how well I did. The day started poorly—drizzling, the mucky streets threatening the cleanliness of my boots and skirt bottom. I had to walk halfway across town to where I could catch the crowded streetcar up to 14th Street. From there, I hurried over to Union Square, to the department's squat brick building. Just inside, people pushed past as I dabbed my wet face, trying to muster my confidence. I strode purposefully into the wide hall, though I wasn't sure where I was going. On the first door to the left, stencilled on the glass, I saw his name, my interviewer, Mr. George Soper, Sanitary Engineer. I stood for a moment, trying to gather my nerve. Across the hall, behind a windowed doorway, I could see the busy activity of men who thankfully took no notice of me.

I knocked and entered my interviewer's office. He was sitting behind his desk and looked remarkably like Mr. Robert Peary, even down to his dark mustache and the part in his hair and the very straight line of his jaw.

He indicated the coatrack; I hung my damp hat and cape. He bowed his head and said, "Please take a seat."

To his right was a desk; on it, a brand-new Remington typing machine. I sat behind it. The size of the deep wooden desk nearly overwhelmed me—I wondered if I had what it took to fill the position. I felt as if my mouth were stuffed with rags, and my back soaked by rain showers.

"Please type these paragraphs," he said, handing me a sheet of paper. He took out a pocket watch. He nodded, and I swallowed the nugget of fear in my throat.

My clothes felt tight and my hands weak as I performed on the stiff new keys. In one minute, he stopped me. He pulled the page out of the machine. He glanced at it, laid it on his desk, and sat down.

I stared at the strong bone of his jaw, the muscle flexing there. I looked at his smoothly oiled hair, his crisp bowtie. I wondered what sort of home he lived in, and what his wife might look like, if he had one.

Beneath his brow, he seemed to be studying me as well.

He tapped his desk slowly with his finger. "Your letter to me was a fine specimen of handwriting," he said.

"Thank you, sir," I said.

"This work demands a good hand," he said.

"Yes, sir."

He cleared his throat and picked up my typing test. I raked my mind for a way to ask him about the job and what it might entail—I tried to call up words, but they seemed as ephemeral as clouds.

"So, I have all of your information, name, address, and such," he said. He stood, as if to end the meeting.

And then it came to me.

"Sir, did the Department of Health and Sanitation begin after Jacob Riis published his book *How the Other Half Lives?*"

His eyes flickered to life then, as if I had brought him out of a dull routine.

"Twenty years ago, the department was in its infancy," he said. "We didn't have such a branch for sanitation."

"I've always been interested in, well, in fighting death," I said. I clutched my own hands, not daring to wipe the sweat from my upper lip.

"The causes of death are many," he said. "Disease, ill health, accidents, childbirth."

"My mother is a midwife," I said, "and I assist her, and often I watch those girls suffer—and my brother—I want to learn, sir, I want to know what makes people ill, what causes sores to become infected, why people bleed, why they die."

I felt unable to stop this horrible declaration of my most morbid thoughts, but the man nodded, looking at me pensively.

"Perhaps I should show you our laboratory," he said. "It's where we do all our experiments and sample testing. You'd be working often with the science fellows, so perhaps you should see. Come, it's just down the hall."

I followed him to the other end of the hall, into the laboratory, a giant room, astonishing in its size and complication—dozens of tools and test tubes and microscopes, things I wanted to touch and look at. I could smell chemicals burning in the beakers. A good number of science fellows bent over tables, their work occupying them until I passed with Mr. Soper. As I listened to my interviewer, I felt watched. I felt aware of my face and hair, I felt light and off balance. I don't think I'd ever been in a room with so many boys before.

I forced myself to focus on Mr. Soper's words.

He stopped at a microscope and tapped it. He said, "Every living thing in the world is made up of tiny cells that are invisible to the bare eye, cells one can see only through a microscope."

I thought of the article I had read with Marm about Dr. Golgi and the nervous cells. I thought of the science book my father gave me.

I felt, listening to my interviewer, as if a door opened just a crack, and I could see the edge of a new world. I wanted to ask if I could look through the bronze microscope he touched and see how we are held together. I wanted to stay in that room for the rest of the day and explore like an arctic adventurer.

"A microscope is just one of the many tools we use," he said. "My position at the department is head epidemiologist, and a large part of our work is investigating the causes of disease epidemics. We want to know how these things start."

This struck me—that there exists a person who searches for the start of disease. Not a doctor, but more like a detective, sifting through scientific evidence.

"I'm ready, sir, to help you in any way I can," I said.

"Good," he said.

I think I saw in him a smile.

He had to return to work; we went back to his office and he offered to pay me five dollars weekly, if hired. That is more money than I ever had—it would make our lives a good bit easier! We closed the meeting with a firm handshake. He said he'd notify me of his decision by next week. It seems I'm not the only person available to do this job, but I know I'm certainly the most interested!

September 30, 1906

Sometimes I get this feeling that I am unable to be sure that everyone around me is seeing the same thing as me. Perhaps it's because I feel I'm the only girl who seems to care about things like disease and death, cells and bones. I feel as if I'm making the world up as I go. Like things aren't real, apart from me. It's very disorienting and a little scary to feel this way, and I'm not sure where it comes from. It's almost as if I'm in a glass beaker alone, unable to touch the world or talk to anyone in it.

There are days, whole days in school that I find I don't remember. I drift along, thinking of other things, the lessons passing through my fingers, into my notepad. I come home and look at my notes and don't recall hearing a word, no less writing any of it. Last semester was terrible. After Anushka left, I felt like a dried insect in a spiderweb, the juice drained from me. I wish there was a school for girls like me, girls interested in the invisible, the biologic, the organic. When I say the word biologic to someone like Josephine, her eyes cross a little, and her mouth gapes, and I can hear her little brain rattling around in her skull like a smooth marble.

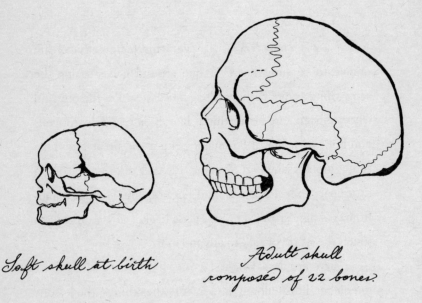

Soft skull at birth

Adult skull composed of 22 bones.

October 5, 1906

I fear I did not get the job. I don't know what happened. I've checked the mailbox every day; I simply never received a notice from my interviewer. I don't want to think about it anymore, but I cannot keep my mind from wandering to it. Marm says I should go up there and inquire, as the man said he would notify me either way. But I wouldn't be able to look into my interviewer's aloof eyes as he rejected me in person. I can hardly believe it. He seemed so pleased with me, my questions, my skills. Every time I think about it, which I do at least a hundred times a day, my other thoughts grow pale and watery until they wash away altogether, and I think once more, *I don't believe I didn't get the job.*

I worry that without it, I will never understand the world, and why terrible things happen to innocent people. This week, death struck again, and I could do nothing to stop it. Hilda

Rothkopf over on Greene Street, a girl who was in my school a few years ahead of me, who used to be Hilda Groenig and is now married to Gerry Rothkopf, who works as a draper on the Ladies' Mile, was with child. Marm had been watching over her the last few months; she finally came due and sent Gerry over. I was home, so I went with Marm to Greene Street, where Hilda's water had broken and she'd entered hard labor. It seems the baby was a breech, and in Marm's experience, the only way to really deliver a breech is to turn it around. Marm rolled up her sleeves, washed her hands and forceps, then set to work turning the baby. My heart dropped for that poor girl, her face twisted in pain. When they heard her cries, sympathetic women neighbors came calling to offer help. It took us nearly an hour to turn the baby. Finally Marm ordered Hilda to push, which she did for the better part of the night, until her baby came out. Tears blinded my eyes when I saw the blue little thing in the basin. I knew immediately that it was dead.

Nine months and the poor girl delivers a stillborn. Such things make me want to wail and shout at the sky! Why didn't that baby survive? Why does death happen to one so young? Why don't we understand the human body?

But I am speechless, weighed down by a heavy sadness. There is no one I can talk to about the why.

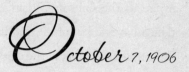
October 7, 1906

I wrote to Anushka and told her my fears about not getting the job, and then I received a letter from her about a lamb she killed, parts of which they cured, and parts they ate for dinner. I feel like my best friend is drifting further and further away from me. Our letters seem to cross, we rarely address one another directly. Finally, today, she wrote asking if I got the job, which caused a cry of frustration in me. If only our letters could reach each other more quickly, the distance between us would not seem so far.

I think I'm just nervous with the waiting—I've applied for other jobs but have heard nothing. Marm says the man still might write to me, but I'm finding that very hard to believe.

Maybe, too, I feel jealous of Anushka's life. She seems to be on a path of adventure and wonder, all sorts of new things happening to her, and here I am, stuck at Mrs. Browning's School for Girls, with no prospects for decent work. Today our short, stout, overly perfumed Miss Ruben told us we should aspire to the Gibson Girl image and think of ourselves as delicate roses. Josephine and Fanny were chosen to walk on their tiptoes in front of the class, in their best refined manner. They did look beautiful on the surface, perfect like pictures. Miss Ruben said that together they looked like a stunning bouquet. "Not like you," she said, turning to me with a dramatic wave of her hand. I sat by the window daydreaming; her attention woke me like a splash of cold water.

"Prudence," she said, "you don't seem to have an ounce of fashion sense. You must loosen, soften. With your hair tied so tightly to your head, you look nothing like a rose. Instead you resemble a prickly, twiggy thistle!"

I felt my heart turn to stone. I heard the other girls tittering. Out of all of them, she had plucked me like a weed to chastise. I wanted to be anywhere but there. I glanced out the window and imagined myself growing in a field of thistles with Anushka, whom I pictured to be the same sort of purple flower as me.

I decided I'd rather be a thistle than a rose. Thistles are vibrant and resilient.

I spent the rest of the day mourning the absence of my Anushka, my best friend who used to sit next to me, passing me smiles throughout our silly lessons.

She writes to me that she hurt her shoulder shooting a rifle. A rifle! How can I answer that, when I have never touched a weapon? She writes about skinning an animal, plucking a chicken, riding a horse bareback, milking a goat with one hand. Shooting a lamb. And I fear we are becoming two completely different people who will never share a common bond again.

But I don't want to lose her.

She is still the girl whose smile I think of whenever I need some cheer.

Cirsium Vulgare
(Thistle)

October 12, 1906

Finally, finally, finally! A miracle has happened, finally, to me! Late this week, I received notice in the mail from my interviewer that I was indeed chosen to be his assistant. He asked me to meet him at his office on Friday to talk about the job. I was so happy to see him again, to look into his serious face, I could barely contain my joy.

I stood at his desk, my hat in hand, watching the strong muscles twitch in his jaw.

"Miss Galewski," he said, "before you agree to take on this work, I would like to make it clear to you that I'm not hiring you as a secretary. Instead I'm looking for someone who can come with me to disease sites and help me investigate causes."

His words frightened me for a moment; I told him I was not any kind of expert.

He shook his head. "I need an assistant, a note taker

who can also be a participant. I'm asking you to use your brain, not just type out the words I dictate, but help me think through the cases."

The description thrilled the words from me; I could only nod in agreement.

He handed me a folio in which to take notes. He said, "The office has just been engaged in a typhoid fever investigation. I'll need your services immediately. Monday at eight in the ante meridiem, we will meet at the office and ride a motor carriage out to Long Island, where a household has taken ill with the disease."

I thought of Marm and school and found myself unable to remind him of my half-day responsibility to attend.

"Sir, I will be here Monday at eight," I said.

He explained that he'd been away on an epidemic hunt, which was why I spent the last intolerable weeks awaiting word from him. Up in Peekskill, he tested water pipes—those running into and out of houses; he traced their path all the way back to the city's reservoir. That reservoir provides Peekskill with its drinking water. There, Mr. Soper discovered that a builder was allowing his workers to bathe and defecate in the reservoir, thus tainting the drinking water. Nearly the whole town contracted the cholera. A number of the weaker Peekskillers, due to excessive diarrhea and vomiting (I must get used to these medical words, as my interviewer uses them freely), mostly young children and elderly folks, died of dehydration.

I didn't show my emotion, but a part of me cringed to hear him talk of the deaths—and I questioned myself—do I really want to take on another job that includes such sorrow? When things go badly, when our mothers or babies die, a wild sadness comes over me, a feeling I can't shake for days.

But this job will be different. Here I'll be taking steps to fight death.

He dismissed me then, and I left the office charged with a sense of awe—at the job, at the man who entrusted it to me. He holds tight his mustachioed face, his moody, watchful eyes closed to me. He has a darkness about him, no doubt from witnessing so much illness, but beneath that seems to lie a great caring.

When I arrived home, I told Marm about our meeting. She immediately objected to the work hours and the travel. I could see it striking her, the turn of her mouth changing, the pinch surfacing on her brow.

"Don't you have to be in school at eight in the morning?" she asked.

When I told Marm that I'd promised to meet Mr. Soper,

she said, "Prudence, the rules of your school state that you may take an afternoon position. You cannot be there in the morning. You must tell him that." She folded her arms. "And I don't like you going in a motor carriage with a stranger, a grown man."

I felt the job slipping away from me at Marm's protests. I saw the reason for her doubts, but I want—I need—the job, so I argued with her.

"If I were a boy—"

"You're not a boy! You're a girl, in her last year of school. This is not what we agreed on!" Marm raised her voice; I don't hear her shout often, and never at me.

"But I want this job! More, much more than school!" I cried.

Marm lowered her eyelids at me. She has worked for years to maintain my standing in that school. She tends to expectant mothers for months only to collect a small sum at the birthing session. Then every fall and spring, she has to pay for my school clothes and for the boots I wear. Money for books and pencils and paper. And she never complains. She thinks it's worth it, that it's a finer school than any of the Free Schools, and that it will lead me to a better job than hers one day.

But I pressed on. "I don't learn anything, Marm! Just bookkeeping, and French, and how to order a household of servants—"

"There's no work for girls in the sciences," she insisted. She struck the table with the flat of her hand and said, "You absolutely cannot take that job. I will not allow it, Prudence!"

I burst out, "If I were a boy like Benny, you would let me take it."

I saw her suck in her breath, as if I had hit her.

"Marm," I cried. "Marm, please!"

I was sorry I had brought up Benny, but I had to make her understand.

She stared at me, her lips pressed so hard together they turned white.

I softened my voice. "Benny is the reason I want the job, Marm. I need to know why he died—I need to understand."

Marm stood so still, I was afraid she had stopped breathing.

I asked her if we could talk to Mrs. Browning. Perhaps we could convince her to allow me to finish lessons on my own time, to remain in school. It was such a rare chance. I brought up Jacob Riis, and all the good things the Department of Health and Sanitation has done for this city.

I clutched my hands together and waited.

Marm said, finally, "We will go see Mrs. Browning privately, and hear what she says. But you must listen to her verdict. If she does not agree, you must stay in school."

I hugged my own waist and held in my reply; Marm turned away from me and started supper, and we spoke no more of it.

We have a meeting with Mrs. Browning this evening in her parlor.

I can't help it; I feel angry at Marm. *She* was the one who taught me about the body and illness, she encouraged me to use my brain, she showed me how to pry into scientific matters, to be curious, always. Now she wants me to be a bookkeeper—why? Most offices hire girls as typists the same way they would buy a vase for flowers; doesn't Marm want me to be smarter than that? My interviewer goes that one step further, he asks me to get my brain involved. It is unusual, I agree, but its very strangeness is what makes it so special.

I feel as if Marm has dropped me from a tall tower, as if she is no longer beside me. I can't find a foothold as to what is right. Take the job and possibly have to leave school, or not take the job and be miserable for the rest of my life. I wish I didn't have to choose between school and work.

October 13, 1906

I took the job, I'm leaving school. I feel as if something inside me has broken, a cord attaching me to a familiar world. I don't know if it's the right thing. So many of our neighborhood girls forgo school to earn money for their families. I hear the Feldman sisters tromping up the stairs and creaking into bed at all hours of the night and have always felt secretly grateful I wasn't in their position. I know I've been held in special esteem by our neighbors, the way Marm has been able to keep me in school. They all thought I would go far, and now I don't know what they'll think.

I must do my best with this job, learn all I can and make something of myself. Maybe I could one day be like Florence Nightingale, a heroic nurse healing the wounded. But she was born into an upper-class English family and could afford to attend the best schools. A future in science seems like such

an impossible dream involving faraway, expensive schools
that certainly would not accept a lower-class American
Jewish girl.

The meeting at Mrs. Browning's has shown me the
shabbiness of my own life.

I got that feeling the moment her maid brought us into
her parlor. I have never been in such an extravagant home.
Hanging from the walls were tiger and lion heads, teeth bared,
eyes glaring. Between two elephant tusks hung photographs
of Mr. Browning with a group of hunters on a safari in Africa.
Another large photo showed Mrs. Browning being hefted in
a conveyance by several men, long peacock feathers decorat-
ing her hat.

Marm sat at the edge of a finely upholstered chair, and
I slipped onto the hard surface of a carved wooden bench.
Crystal lamps shimmered on the side tables, lace curtains
covered the windows. My teacher's home seemed to perfectly
follow the rules of decorative furnishings we'd studied in the
Ladies' Home Journal. Even down to the obese Persian cat
that lay on the Oriental carpet, swishing its tail, watching us
with careful eyes.

Marm played with her purse, popping it and snapping it.
I sat with my hat in hand and stared at the painting of Mary

and Jesus on the far wall. I felt Mrs. Browning had us wait those several minutes in order to fully absorb her providence.

Finally she came in, followed by her butler, with tea. How strange it felt to be served by a real butler. He poured and left us and Mrs. Browning chattered with Marm for a few minutes about what a good student I am, always attentive and so on. Marm looked so out of place. Her usually rosy cheeks were the color of waxed beans, her mouth curved downward. She was unhappy with me for wanting to leave school; she was not comfortable in this woman's house, forced into the position of having to barter for me. It made me angry to read all this in her face.

"It's very lovely to speak with you, Mrs. Galewski, but you must remind me what brought your visit," Mrs. Browning said.

Marm cleared her throat and said, "It seems Prudence has managed to find a sort of job. She would be working at the New York City Department of Health and Sanitation, assisting a sanitary engineer."

My bright teacher turned to me, nose wrinkled, her perfectly plucked brows furrowed. She said, "A sanitary engineer? Why would you want to assist such a person, Prudence?"

The question felt like a pin through my stomach. She

had rarely spoken directly to me before, except to tell me how pretty I'd be if only I put my hair in curls and wore a ribbon in my collar.

"Mrs. Browning," I said, "I've been working as Marm's assistant through the whole summer."

I glanced at Marm, thinking of our argument about Mr. Soper choosing me.

I pushed on: "I thought my mother was satisfied with me as assistant, even though I am only sixteen and a girl."

A blush spread on Marm's cheeks, anger and embarrassment at my bringing our private argument about my interviewer to the public.

I pushed myself to continue, to fight for this job: "Mrs. Browning, I feel inside me a need to expand my knowledge, to learn more about how the human body functions, and I think this job assisting the head epidemiologist would help me do just that."

Mrs. Browning's eyes pressed into me like little thumbs. She said, "I'm surprised at your choice for your life, Prudence. I thought after graduation that you would seek work as a secretary, and not muck about in human filth. A girl with your skill could acquire respectable employment at one of the finer banks in the city. You could work up to private secretary for the bank manager. Or perhaps keep books at one of the fashion houses. Even governess for royalty. Proper work," she said, "for which we've prepared you."

The thought of being in one of those jobs, counting other people's money or watching their babies all day, nearly choked me. I looked at Marm, then back at my teacher, who nodded at me to speak.

"I have learned a great deal at your school, Mrs. Browning," I said.

Her expectant eyes didn't leave me, so I went on, "The work for Mr. Soper would challenge me."

Mrs. Browning asked me what exactly I meant by that.

"I will not simply be a witness to death," I said. "In working with Mr. Soper to find the source of disease, I will be helping to stop its spread. I feel that it's an important job."

The tips of her nostrils flared. "And why does this man want *your* help? A young girl like you? Can't he find a budding science fellow to do the work?"

I felt my own eyes open like tea saucers. I wanted to shout, *I am a budding scientist! He saw that in me, why can't you see the same?* But she didn't see me as anything more than a girl, that was the problem, it had always been the problem. I held in the fury that twisted around my heart like rope.

Instead I quietly replied, "He hired me as typist and note taker. It was only afterwards that he called me assistant."

An awfully wry smile spread over Mrs. Browning's face. "Beyond typing, what exactly are your tasks?" she asked.

"I don't know. Mr. Soper will teach me when I begin," I said.

"For example, will you *cure* the *disease?*" She smiled and tilted her head.

I didn't like her implications one bit. I repeated slowly, "I will help to stop its spread, ma'am."

That gave her pause. She sipped her tea and nibbled a ladyfinger, and I felt the relief of her wide gray stare removed from me, only to turn and catch Marm, the dull, unhappy look in her eyes changed to a curious sort of pride.

"And so what is the problem?" Mrs. Browning asked. "You know that you can work at any job you like."

"He expects me there at eight in the morning," I told her.

"Ah," she said. She sniffed her tea and put it down and wiped her fingertips on her satin napkin. "You know my rules," she said.

Marm spoke up, surprising me. "Mrs. Browning," she said, "can't you consider giving Prudence credit for doing such a worthy job? Surely you could overlook the rules this one time and allow her to make up the lessons nights and weekends."

My eyes stung salty when I felt Marm at my side once again. I told Mrs. Browning I'd do any work she asked.

"Jealousy is a large commodity at our school, you know that, Prudence. Rules are created to keep order," Mrs. Browning said. "The girls would not think their education was very important if I let you work instead of attending school."

"Let's not tell the other girls," I suggested.

"Miss Prudence Galewski," she said, "if you can no longer appreciate the standards of our institution, perhaps I can find another needy girl on whom I can bestow the donated funds that you currently enjoy."

I never saw my missus so frosty before.

"Do you not own the school, Mrs. Browning?" Marm broke in. "Can you not consider for one moment the rare situation my daughter is in? For once, a man in high position has recognized a girl's talent, and is willing to give her a chance to use it. I don't understand why you won't help Prudence, why you can't see the opportunity being offered to her!"

"I'm afraid *you* do not see what is before you," Mrs.

Browning huffed. "The opposite sex stands ready to take advantage of your daughter, and you are ushering her straight into such difficulty!"

"I beg your pardon!" Marm exclaimed, jumping out of her chair. "Prudence is the most important person in the world to me, and if I thought she would come to harm in any way, I would not let her work in that office. But I am proud of my daughter for her intelligence and bravery, and I am sorry you don't feel the same way. Good night to you, ma'am!"

She took my wrist and we walked out. It was all so horrible.

And now I'm not in school anymore.

I hope I have made the right decision.

October 19, 1906

Today was my first day of work with Mr. Soper. It was disorienting for me to rise with the church bells and get ready for work instead of preparing for school. I felt confused, and didn't know what was appropriate dress for my first ride in a motor carriage as my wardrobe consists mainly of my simple black school skirts and white shirtwaists and jackets. Would I need something more professional, like a suit? I didn't know what an assistant was supposed to look or act like. I wasn't sure I would be able to meet my chief's expectations. Mrs. Browning's doubts sounded in my head, but I put on my good maroon outfit with matching cape and hat and made myself walk the whole mile to work as walking always calms me.

I met Mr. Soper at the office, where he waited outside in the crisp morning air with Mr. Thompson, our round, balding

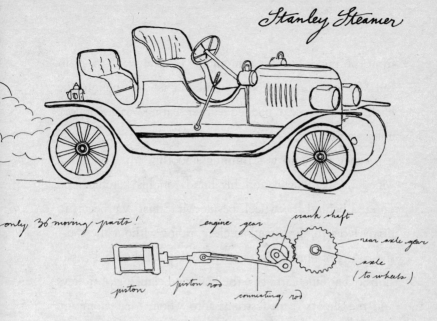

Stanley Steamer

only 36 moving parts!

engine gear | crank shaft | rear axle gear | axle (to wheels)

piston | piston rod | connecting rod

client. They both leaned on one of those Stanley Steamers I've seen advertised on billboards near Tin Pan Alley. When Mr. Soper saw me, he nodded to Mr. Thompson, who went to the front of the motor carriage, opened the hood, and began to do something with the engine. I had never been so close to an actual locomobile—they're always passing so rapidly on the streets, and seem so unstable, as if they may explode any second. This one was grass green with white spoked wheels and a black top, neatly folded down. It shone so brightly, I felt myself drawn to touch the vehicle. The coach came to life with a spit and a roar, and I jumped back, feeling as if a friendly dog had suddenly barked at me. Vapor emanated from the hood, and for a moment, I didn't want to go in. But Mr. Soper reached out a hand and assisted me into the back. The expanse of padded leather seating was as comfortable as a sofa.

Once the auto was running smoothly, Mr. Thompson wiped his bare head and his hands on his kerchief and entered behind the wheel, beside Mr. Soper. We began to drive. Everything seemed so close, riding without the top— the snorts of horses that loomed overhead, the loud explosions of gasoline carriages, the bells and clanging of trolleys, and the shouts of pedestrians into whom Mr. Thompson nearly crashed several times. We flew past everything so quickly, my head spun. I clutched the side of the carriage, trying to steady myself, and held on to my hat, afraid of what I had gotten myself into. Mr. Soper broke off his inaudible shouts to our client and turned to glance at me every now and then, I think to make sure I hadn't been hit by flying debris. I'm ashamed to say it, but secretly I prayed to be back in school, sitting beside Josephine, looking out the window at the smokestacks and thinking my own quiet thoughts. It wasn't until we crossed the grand, jammed Brooklyn Bridge and drove up through Queens and out to more rural lands that I began to enjoy the ride, and the feel of wind on my face. I've never had reason to visit the New York countryside, and the vision of cows munching hay in the fields and the fresh smell of the reddening autumn leaves soothed me.

Mr. Soper is a very serious man, with hardly a moment to explain things to me. At Oyster Bay, on Long Island, we pulled up to a stone mansion surrounded by exotic flowers dying in their pods and ripening apple trees overlooking the water. The country seemed so serene. Mr. Soper got out with Mr. Thompson; they'd been discussing how typhoid could be carried in food, and Mr. Soper wanted to see the kitchen first. I followed them around back. That kitchen was bigger than our entire apartment! Light poured in through four windows and bounced off the shiny bottoms of the dozens of copper pots that hung against the wide brick chimney. I felt myself shifting from foot to foot, distracted by the size and blackness of the stove, the look of the real icebox, the chopping block as long as my bed.

"Pay attention, Miss Galewski, and write this information into the folio!" Mr. Soper barked at me. "Think of what Mr. Thompson is saying."

I quickly opened the folder and gripped my pencil. It was hard to pay attention with so much to look at, but I kept my eyes down on the paper, feeling the blush crawl up my neck.

"This is our situation here," he said. "Mr. Thompson's family and servants first became ill September fourth, write that down, specific notes, his sons fell fevered at ten o'clock on that Thursday morning after eating apples and cheese, the laundress got sick that Sunday at seven in the a.m. after breakfasting on pancakes, stay alert and keep your hand moving. This is your job," he said.

He had heard things I missed completely. I wrote as quickly as I could, trying to keep my mind on my work.

Mr. Soper began to question Mrs. Thompson, who came into the pantry (shelves and shelves filled with cookies and breads and honey and jarred jams, all the food one could ever want). I stood behind him, feeling a bit unsteady, my mouth dry, my stomach empty. Plump Mrs. Thompson's thick yellow hair hung loose in its bun, her skin a rashy pink; clearly, she had barely recovered from the fever. But Mr. Soper questioned her thoroughly just the same.

Her voice wavered as she described how she'd begun feeling sick on a Friday night at eleven p.m. in mid-September (the twelfth, same day as her daughter Amy), after her dinner guests—the McDonnell, Graff, and Chadwell couples (no children)—had departed. (Menu: Broiled sole with asparagus tips. Caviar, chocolate mousse. French bread, butter from a neighboring farm.) Mr. Soper asked her about the visitors, if any of them had fallen ill, or could have brought the disease into the house. She shook her head; her doctors had spoken to their acquaintances (the three couples, plus the Lyons family, Mr. Cerasano, and the neighbors, the Heightons, and their five boys). As far as they knew, her friends had neither brought nor contracted the typhoid.

As she spoke, Mr. Soper made sure I wrote names, foods, times, dates. We will follow these like breadcrumbs through the forest, he says.

Mrs. Thompson then showed us the dining room where most of the family's meals took place, and after, she walked us through the house. I followed her and Mr. Soper through the bedrooms and bathrooms, feeling odd about being in this wealthy family's home, their life so different from mine, their privacy completely revealed to us. I had to keep reminding myself that they had been struck by a terrible disease, and I was there to help find out why.

In the afternoon, we talked briefly to the eldest son, Jimmy, a boy my age, blond like his mother, long-limbed, easy with himself. He had fully healed from the sickness, though I noted the prominence of his collarbones and the greenish tinge under his cheerful blue eyes. He had gone clamming in the bay with his brothers Ronnie and Billy all summer. They had played polo at their neighbor's to the right, the Heightons. The three boys had come down with the illness on the same day (September 4). Mr. Soper asked him to remember when exactly it struck them, and the boy said that it was in the early morning (sometime before the mailman arrived at nine). Not a Friday like Mrs. Thompson; in fact, their illness came more than a week before Mrs. Thompson's.

We left the house after our interview with the boy. Mr. Thompson and Mr. Soper didn't speak on the ride back. At the office, at the end of the day, Mr. Soper nodded to me and said, "There is a depth to this case we're not yet reaching. We will return to Oyster Bay tomorrow. We have a good deal of work ahead of us."

All day, I felt as if things were going on somewhere above me, while I tried to climb high enough to see, to understand. Follow the food, Mr. Soper says, follow the movements of the family—but I feel like I don't know what we're looking for. I don't even know how we'll know when we've found it!

October 23, 1906

The typhoid that spread through the household ended its course by the beginning of this month. I understand now the nature of epidemiology, and Mr. Soper's work: If we don't find out how this fever started, it could resurface, and pass like a plague through water or food or some other means, into the neighborhood. That would be disastrous.

We've gone back to the house each day this week, collecting evidence, building the information we have about this large household. With each visit, I learned more about their lives—Mr. Soper says we must especially focus on the foods they eat, an amount that seems enough to feed everyone on my street.

We interviewed the two maids, the laundress, the gardener, and the butler, all of whom became ill on a Saturday

(September 6), the same week as the boys. Mr. Soper asked each of them to recall what they ate in the last month, and I jotted everything in the folio. It's a most difficult task trying to get eleven people to remember thirty days of eggs and bacon and grits, baked breads and muffins, cheese sandwiches and tomatoes and apples and plums, steaks and potatoes and salads and chops and spaghettis and sauces, desserts and snacks, especially when they don't all join together for each meal, and the servants graze like cows, it seems. My lists are so complex, they'll have to be cross-referenced and indexed like a book. I spent the week working on charts and graphs to order the types of foods together, with headings of Dairy and Meat and Vegetable and so on, but I'm not even halfway through.

I cannot help but wonder what it would be like to have so much food to eat, whenever one wanted to eat it. With an icebox and a pantry, all sorts of things seem possible.

I took notes of the household's movements and developed charts of People Visited, Places Traveled, and Visitors to Home. I feel a little like a spy, writing down who this family goes to meet, and who comes to visit. I think of the social circles Mrs. Browning always had us aspire to—and wonder what she would think of me writing down the eating and visiting habits of the rich.

Mr. Soper inspected the house and collected water from the well, and scrapings from the taps. We took samples of lamb, beef, chicken, and milk, and peaches, apples, bananas, and greens from the kitchen. Out in the backyard, he took a shovel and dug down deep until we reached the smell of sewage, which was the septic field for the house's toilets. He shoveled up samples and bottled them, handing the odiferous tubes to me without worrying about offending my female senses. He put me in charge of labeling and stacking these bottled samples in their wooden holders, and I have to say, I felt a certain joy rolling up my sleeves and performing this dirty work alongside him. We brought the samples back to the laboratory to test for disease, and we now await the results.

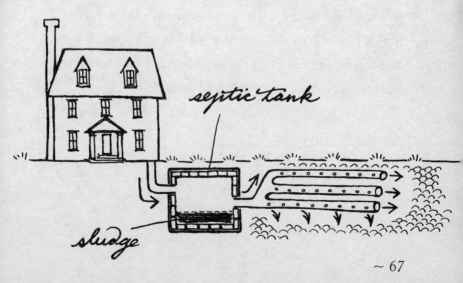

septic tank

sludge

I found out that Mr. Thompson does not own this mansion—he only rents it from a rich merchant for the summer; he's terribly nervous that the merchant is going to blame him for the disease, especially if we don't find the cause. Worst of all, the family is trapped on Long Island and cannot return to their townhouse in the city, as their landlord will not take them if they carry the fever. The children cannot return to school until they are all completely well.

I think the hardest hit by all this was little Amy Thompson, who just came out of Nassau Hospital. A shy child of seven, her long brown hair tied up in a bow, she is neat and polite, normal-seeming, until one looks at her face. It seems a fever rash had broken out over her neck and chin, and she could not let it alone. The itch plagued her, and she scratched and picked and left such awful sores that have not healed properly, patchy scars that will stay with her all her life. In a family portrait on the mantelpiece, I saw that Amy had been a beautiful girl with a bold smile.

I fear the fever has taken her beauty and that easy personality away from her.

October 25, 1906

Mr. Soper and I went to the laboratory where the science fellows studied our samples through their microscopes, and again I felt that strange sensation of being aware of my face and body. It got worse when one of the boys leaned over and whispered as I passed, "Want to look through my microscope?" I felt as if all eyes in the room turned then, and were waiting for me to answer. I stood frozen while I searched my mind for a reply. Mr. Soper didn't hear the boy's words, but sensing his attention on me, snapped at the fellow, "Mind your work, Jonathan!" and the boy lowered his eyes. He had foppish hair and a patch of fur on his chin, looking rather like a he-goat, including the smile on his face. I'm not accustomed to such boldness.

I don't think I have ever known a girl like me who was so very awkward with boys. Even Anushka once had an outing with a feller—Jim McAvoy—though that turned bad when she tried to explain to him her father's idea about the commune and living in nature. Poor Jim had never met a girl who understood such ideas, and never came calling for her again. That gave us both a lesson—don't talk about ideas with boys. Maybe Anushka will have another chance—just yesterday, she wrote of being sweet on a feller named Randall. She met him on the Columbus Day hayride, but she didn't say whether he knew of her feelings or if she's still a secret admirer. She's a girl of mystery when it comes to love. I wrote back, asking what exactly he looks like, and if she's spoken to him in any meaningful manner. I asked her to write the whole love story out for me, dialogue and all. I told her to make it good, as I'd commit her lines to memory, and use them for my own next time a boy tries to speak to me.

Mr. Soper and I took the results of our sample tests to his office to study them. As he rifled through the pages, I did wonder aloud what the world might look like through a microscope, but Mr. Soper did not take my hint. Instead he handed over a section of the laboratory results for me to type out, stained sheets of tables and charts with breakdowns of the samples, all poorly handwritten, with columns and diagrams that I found difficult to understand. Mr. Soper showed me which rows to follow. "We are looking for a positive identification," he said, "something that tells us that the typhoid disease might live in any of the foodstuffs or organic matter we collected."

I examined each page he gave me as I typed it. I had expected at least one source to show positive for the disease, yet they all, every single one, came out clean. When I told him, Mr. Soper double-checked, frustration wrinkling his brow. The information seemed to move him to work harder, to search deeper for an answer to the question before us. We must go back, he says, and ask more pointedly about the family's agenda, what they did, who they saw, how the disease might have traveled into their home.

I'm coming to dislike these drives to Long Island—not the trip, but the way the children run to the door, their mouths expectant and wide, the worried peak of Mrs. Thompson's brow when we return once again having uncovered nothing. It's another day they must remain in the house, away from their city home, and school, and friends.

Strange where clues can come from. After shopping for Mrs. Zanberger one evening (she's now home from the hospital, and acting the perfect invalid), I sat with her in her kitchen, peeling a five-pound sack of potatoes for her as

her hands hurt too much for the work. In the course of the labor, she asked me about my job at the department, and I told her of the case. She said that her cousin got the typhoid once from a bushel of clams he fished out of Sheepshead Bay. Nearly the whole neighborhood had fallen ill with the disease from those clams, she said. I took this report to Mr. Soper, and the information illuminated his eyes, and he shuffled through our notes, saying that bottom-feeding shellfish *was* a common cause of the illness, and that next week we would thoroughly investigate that angle. Warmth gushed through me, pride, I guess, at finally having something to offer.

Lately I seem to think about my father and brother more and more. Not actual thoughts, but pictures. I see them in the boys and men at the office. What Benny might have become. What Papa might look like now. Around the time my father decided to go to Cuba to fight against Spain, I felt a darkness about him, as if a shadow had engulfed him and wouldn't let him go. I think I was confused and so angry at him for signing up to leave us, I couldn't speak, not enough to pierce his darkness. I remember thinking, *What about us?* Over the years, I've invented reasons for his leaving us: Grandfather fought in the Civil War, and maybe that's why my father wanted to fight too. Maybe it was a way for him to feel he could win, after death won the fight with Benny.

Or maybe I will never understand.

Even as I think of my father and brother more, with this new job I feel the emptiness less. My days are filled with work, writing and typing, figuring and organizing, and when I come home, I am eager to spend the evenings and weekends keeping up with my own personal record here in my tablets. The pain of missing Papa and Benny is overtaken by the busyness of my mind and hand. I am grateful to Mr. Soper; the difficulty of the tasks he entrusts to me, every moment of the day my thoughts absorbed by puzzles he presents me. It's the type of work I have needed, the challenge that will help me overcome old sorrows.

November 2, 1906

Marm agreed that the first weeks of my pay should go toward improving my wardrobe, so I went to Macy's and bought three shirtwaists (a mint green, a pale yellow, and peach), and two brown tweed skirts, which are more professional than my school skirts. I used the last of my pennies to surprise Marm with a sliver of her favorite cheesecake from Rosario's Bakery. As I was leaving, I glimpsed a familiar face at one of the tables, sitting alone in front of a giant chocolate bonbon. For a moment I couldn't place her, then of course it struck me; it was Josephine, from school. School has been so far from my thoughts, but upon seeing Jo, it came rushing back to me, the easy company of the girls, the undemanding work.

My unhappiness there.

Wiping the sticky smear from her lips, Jo asked what had

happened to me. It seems Mrs. Browning pretends I never existed, and the girls were talking of coming to my apartment to search for me. Jo asked if I was sick—I think they were afraid I might have died. I told her about Marm's argument with Mrs. Browning, and my new job, and she asked me to help finish off her forbidden delight. She wanted me to go on a trolley ride to Coney Island with her and the girls this Sunday, but I told her of my commitment to spend the day catching up in my tablet. I tried to explain how important my notes were to me, then stopped when I saw her eyes drifting. She mentioned her engagement to Will Stryker, the marriage date set for a month from now. When I inquired why the wedding was so soon, a sunrise pinked her cheek, and I asked the poor girl no more questions.

Seeing so many girls who are nearly my age having babies, it makes me think—will I ever have one? I have thought it through, and for three reasons, I feel childbearing distant from me: (1) because I've seen the pain of birth, and the rate of death alarms me—until I know more about why mothers and babies die, I wouldn't take such a step; (2) I want to have my life to myself, and not give it away to a helpless creature who needs me at every turn: food, comfort, bath, shelter; and (3) while I would be curious to observe the process of a child growing inside me (cell by cell?), the thought of its flesh and bones and muscles pushing me outward to make room for itself makes me somewhat queasy.

I talked my thoughts over with Marm, and she was quiet. Then she said I felt that way because I had not found a beau to love. I could nearly touch her soreness, the way my father left us. And I wonder if it's true: Do I not dare to love someone the way other girls my age do? When I think of love with a boy, that place in my chest tenses, and the question comes: If I loved someone, if I allowed that sort of warmth into my heart, would he go away?

My solitude at times is overwhelming, but I fear the pain of loss is worse.

November 5, 1906

After our inconclusive test results, Mr. Soper and I traveled to Long Island once again to speak with the family and servants, and to visit farms and food establishments nearby the house.

An old Indian woman with two long braids and colorful embroidered clothing lives in a tent by the shore and sells shellfish to all of Oyster Bay. She let us take some samples of her goods but pointed out that if her foodstuffs were tainted, the whole neighborhood would've become ill. Mr. Soper asked if she fished the waters alone, or if she worked with anyone else along the bay who might have sold the family shellfish. The strange woman said she worked alone, she sold alone, and nobody got fevered from her fish. We checked the medical records in the neighborhood, and she was right. Families contracted consumption, a pox, and polio, but no one else in Oyster Bay got typhoid this summer.

We took the fish samples and visited two farms in the area. I've never had the opportunity to stand beside a group of cows before—the size and smell of them overwhelmed me. They seemed so odd, with their watery eyes, the flatness of their furred heads banging the stalls to draw my attention, their long tongues hanging out, mouths dripping with saliva. Chickens ran underfoot; low-bellied cats slinked after them. At the lamb stalls, looking at those pink-nosed innocents, a pang of guilt struck me. I thought of Anushka aiming her rifle at one of those animals, I thought of their skins being removed, their bodies being quartered and stewed. I wonder—are we spoiled, here in the city? I have eaten many a lamb stew, but I buy the stock at Mr. Barren's. I never meet with the animal eye-to-eye.

I think living so near the very creatures she consumes has changed Anushka's life. It gave me a glimmer, being on those farms, of the vast difference between the life of a city girl and that of a country girl. How she's had to adapt! What will my visit be like, I wonder.

Will we have the same bond after so much time apart?

November 7, 1906

I discovered the most incredible coincidence, one that blew through me like a tempest. In typing his old notes, I found that the first fever case Mr. Soper ever investigated took him to Cuba in 1898, the year of our war against Spain. I stared at the page when I read that.

Mr. Soper and my father were in Cuba at the very same time.

How shocking, that he might have crossed paths with Papa! I long to ask if Mr. Soper knows anything about him, but it's not a question I feel I can voice—it's too close, too private to discuss.

I'm afraid it might seem like my father ran off and left us.

I must calm this storm inside me. Mr. Soper could have some very important information about Papa—he could know where he is!

I will wait—one day the time will come, the right time will come to ask him. Now is not that time.

Mr. Soper has been working for years to keep epidemics at bay, even in the face of the impossibility of completely ridding humanity of disease. He wants me to learn from his previous examples by transcribing and ordering all of his past cases, which is quite a task, considering how poor the penmanship is of these records—small, tight lettering, words in every margin, drawn maps blotched with ink, all written by Mr. Soper himself. Such a perfect man in every other respect—looking at his handwriting, I feel as if I've discovered a large tear in a very expensive suit. No wonder he sought to hire a girl who knows how to use quill and typing machine.

In Cuba my chief observed the men and realized that the yellow fever spread by contagion: The soldiers fought so closely together, sharing food and water, that they gave each other the sickness. That's when Mr. Soper did something truly revolutionary: He set up a method of separation, keeping the sick apart from the healthy to check the growth of what is called bacteria. I am beginning to understand that it's these bacteria, or germs, that cause disease. He called this method of germ-killing "anti-sepsis."

I do wonder what bacteria might look like, and how they might travel from person to person as in a contagion.

There were other fever epidemics—thirteen hundred people ill in 1903, six hundred in 1904. I guess we are lucky to have only nine sick, none dead, in our typhoid case. Mr. Soper says he doesn't think the household members of the Thompson family gave the disease to each other the way the soldiers did. He says because the Thompsons came down with the typhoid at nearly the same time, each person must have contracted the disease from an individual source such as a food or water. This makes sense to me.

I see so much of him in the old records, Mr. Soper, the way his mind works, tearing each new bit of information apart, breaking it down to smaller pieces to look at it more closely, to wonder about it and worry it like a sore tooth. He has a mind that doesn't easily let go of things, not without fully understanding them first. That's why he's so good at his job; that's why I'm so glad I can watch and learn from him and listen to his deep voice explaining difficult things to me every day.

November 8, 1906

Odd morning.

In working so closely with men, encountering them daily, watching how they behave with each other, and with me, I have to wonder at our differences. We are made to fit together like two halves that combine into a whole. Our minds are supposed to complement each other, women nurture, men provide, yet this design of nature dismays me; it seems so flawed. It often seems that we are as mismatched as horses and rabbits. If it were meant to be, our togetherness, why is it so difficult?

I'm thinking of this today both because of the letter I received from Anushka, and because of a chance meeting this morning between myself and that peculiar science fellow who works in the laboratory, the one who asked me to look at his microscope. I felt eyes upon me as I was purchasing a basket of eggs from the lady on Hester. There he was, holding a paper he'd plucked from the newsie, staring at me from its pages. He has a way of looking at me that seems far too open and familiar to be proper.

He greeted me too informally as well: "Fancy meeting you here, Prudence," he said.

His steady gaze made my stomach hurt, but I nodded politely.

"I live on Essex," he said. "I live alone."

The implications of that frightened me. I started to walk away when he stopped me: "Hey, you know, you weren't the only one who applied for the job as Soper's assistant. My friend did too, and he should've gotten it. He's like me, a science fellow."

My breath caught in my throat. I hadn't heard about anyone else in our department applying for the job. I wasn't sure he was telling the truth.

The boy went on: "Mr. Soper gave it to you because he likes to be around pretty girls."

I felt as if he insulted me in his feeble attempt to flatter me. I turned to face this wicked boy fully and asked, "Can your friend type forty words per minute, write in a neat hand under pressure, *and* dig into a septic field?"

He burst out laughing. I quickly turned and hurried away from him.

I don't think I've ever experienced a young man's attention like that, the way he seemed to look right through me. And I believe he used that lie about the other science fellow just to inflame me.

Poor Anushka—she isn't properly prepared to conduct herself around fellers either, it seems. She writes that her friend Ida has confessed that she too loves this Randall person, but didn't tell Anushka for fear it would ruin their friendship. I ask: Is this new friend even worth keeping? Apparently, Ida did know of Anushka's feelings before she announced hers, but she still loves him anyway and cannot keep it inside. I think, if they are both truly in love with the same boy, they should bring the dilemma to Randall himself. Let the feelings come to a boil, push them to the outer limit of expression, pour the salt into the wound, a painful but rapid solution. In the end, anyway, he will be the one to choose between the two young ladies.

Besides, I'm not so sure fellers are worth all the suffering. I'm really not sure at all.

November 11, 1906

I've been working in the office past seven p.m., typing out my copious notes to make them clear for Mr. Soper to read each morning. In each chart, we have food separations—dairy, meats, vegetables, fruits; and baked goods; and foods fried, boiled, frozen; and who ate what, and when. One item keeps cross-referencing, fitting into dairy, fruit, and frozen, and evening meals, snacks, and even breakfast—I notice it keeps appearing more frequently than the others. I noted times and dates, and it seems that everyone in the family, without exception, ate peach ice cream sometime within the week preceding their illness.

I showed Mr. Soper the charts and how popular peach ice cream was at the Thompsons', and such a pleased light shone from his eyes, it took my breath away. It makes me smile to think of it now. He says we will follow this lead next week.

Sometimes I have the most unusual feeling at the office, a forgetting of myself that happens when I am deep into the work of transcribing notes. I feel as if I am no longer me, but rather part of a larger thing, a giant machine with many components that functions perfectly. A machine of knowledge, one that moves our lives forward in important ways. It's those times when I'm furthering our work that I am happiest.

Marm, however, seems to be in low spirits. I worry she's becoming lonely without me around so often. I've arrived at the apartment after normal hours thinking it's empty. The front room where I write beside the window and sleep by the stove and where we keep our kitchen and bathing things is quiet and untouched, and the little back room where Marm sleeps is darkened. Evenings, when we are both home, we usually sit at our wooden table, boiling rose tea in which to dip the day-old bread that complements a warmed, fragrant spread of salted schmaltz, sharing our borrowed newspaper or occasional magazine by gaslight. Nights when I'm late, there have been no cooking smells wafting through the rooms, and I find Marm asleep in the dark back room. She stirs when she hears me, and when she comes out, I see her eyes puffy and red, and her hair loose. Her natural beauty seems blunted then, the pretty pink of her lips and cheeks faded. It shakes me, seeing her like that, and I ask if anything is bothering her, but she claims not, and bustles about, lighting the stove and warming the chicken fat and the bread. She feeds me and asks me lots of questions about my work. She especially asks about Mr. Soper, and his behavior toward me, as if she still hears Mrs. Browning's ugly parting words. I tell her Mr. Soper has more concern for the sewage system than for the female species. I talk about our case. Tonight I described the very possible breakthrough we may have, thanks to the clue of the peach ice cream. The more I spoke to her, the more she relaxed, and smiled, and even seemed satisfied we had made the right decision.

I worry my work life will take me too far from my home life, like those characters in the novel I've been reading, *The Jungle*, by Mr. Sinclair. It's a terrifying story, yet it feels true—the Lithuanian immigrants remind me very much of my more troubled neighbors: Too many overworked foreigners living on top of each other, sharing customs and the stink of boiled cabbage in the hallway. How lucky Marm and I are to have our little cubby of an apartment all to ourselves. I don't envy the difficulty my neighbors experience when they come to a new country where they don't speak the language and don't know the customs and sometimes have to hide their religion. We all seem to be from somewhere else, except of course the

Indians, and in their exotic dress and features, they appear the most foreign of all to me.

I feel like things are changing for me and Marm, the way the light does through the seasons, rays becoming whiter in winter, thinning out, separating. We don't have enough time together anymore—though we have more money because of my job, we haven't had any outings at all. I wish I could *be more* for Marm, *do more* for her—I think she is getting older and more tired. I must make an effort to spend time with her, if I can.

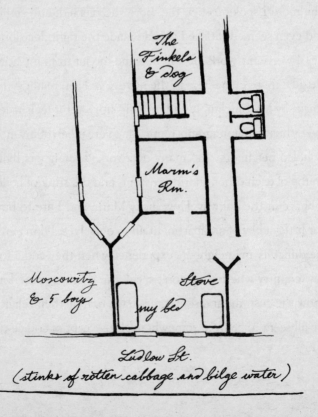

The
Finkels
& dog

Marm's
Rm.

Moscowitz
& 5 boys

Stove

my bed

Ludlow St.
(stinks of rotten cabbage and bilge water)

November 14, 1906

I'm not sure how it happened, but it appears that the strange science fellow has found himself seriously interested in me, though I can't say I return the feeling. He has waited after work to walk me home twice this week, to my great embarrassment. I don't want Mr. Soper to see me associating with him; I don't think my chief likes this boy much. I have turned him down, yet he follows me like a pup. His stare troubles me, and the prospect of his touch is distasteful. I suppose the best I can do is to ignore him, and perhaps he'll leave me be.

November 16, 1906

It turns out that there was a cook who worked for the family back in August that none of the Thompson household had thought to mention. When we asked specifically about the peach ice cream, they all remembered this woman as the one who made it. Mrs. Thompson went over her housekeeping records for us and came across the woman's information. She said her name was Mary Mallon, and described her as fortyish, tall, heavy, Irish from Ireland, in perfect health, and not known to have ever had an attack of the typhoid. She was not a person of many words. Apparently, she kept to herself, quietly cooking adequate meals and retiring to her room when her job was done. She did not stand out in anyone's mind (except for the ice cream), and left after three weeks, just after the illness hit.

Mr. Soper thinks this cook Mary may very well be the

key to our case. There's one problem: We can't find her. It seems she changed employment bureaus, and the one who hired her out to the Thompson family hasn't heard from her. They sent us over to Mrs. Cleanglove's Handy Helpers, but they have not seen her either. The man at Handy Helpers was very forthcoming and gave us a list of residences where she has worked for him in the last five years. Mr. Soper wonders if she has taken ill, or has left the city, in which case our whole lead may fall apart. He says Monday we will begin with a concerted search for this woman, physically traveling house to house until we find her.

The cook has no record of the typhoid, nor any significant illness, so I'm not sure I understand exactly why Mr. Soper suspects she is at the heart of our case. Usually typhoid is carried by a person who suffers from the disease. If this woman didn't become ill at the Thompsons', and never contracted the fever, I don't follow Mr. Soper's line of thought.

I fear we may be traversing down another dead end.

November 23, 1906

White ribbons snake into my heart as our work progresses, deathly white ribbons that frighten me.

We started off the search for Mary Mallon with the only information available to us—the record of the families the cook worked for over the last five years. We took upon ourselves the task of visiting every household on the list. Mr. Soper wanted to know if they remembered the cook, and if they knew anything about her past, or her present whereabouts.

I feared a blind search that would yield nothing. Who would remember a cook from five years past, and why would they keep track of her? And how would we explain our purpose in looking for a woman who's never been sick, but who supposedly carries disease?

But Mr. Soper's instincts were right.

At the first house, a surly maidservant answered, and my chief introduced himself and explained that we were from the Department of Health and Sanitation and were looking for one Mary Mallon. The girl's face shuttered completely, and she said she didn't know anything about the cook. It happened to us more than once this week. I think there is some code of silence among these servants: The moment they sense trouble, their entire countenance snaps shut like an irritated clam. Once their masters are retrieved, the true story arises. Her lady came down the stairs, and when we put to her the same inquiry, her eyes brightened. "Why, of course, Mary Mallon," she exclaimed, "she was such a darling help when the children were ill." She turned to her maid and said, "You remember, Sally, you were ill too, and Mary nursed you to health."

Mr. Soper asked, "What illness?"

The lady answered, "Why, the typhoid fever. It came not long after Mary, maybe two or three weeks later, I guess. It was late fall of that year, and as cold outside as a chicken's beak. She stayed with us for about six months, till the spring of 1903, when we moved here. For an Irish girl, she was quite the angel. The children loved her."

I could see Mr. Soper pale. He asked how many in the

household had fallen ill, and she counted on her fingers, her two children, the maid, and the laundress.

"Did they all recover?" he asked.

"Why, yes," she said.

He asked if the lady knew of Mary's present whereabouts, but she did not. She mentioned another employment bureau that placed the cook in her next job. She asked if we needed a recommendation for Mary's services, which she'd be happy to provide. Mr. Soper politely declined. We bid the woman good day and left.

Riding the elevated train to the next family on our list, I think we were both too surprised to say anything. It felt as if Mr. Soper's idea had been proven—not a good feeling— quite terrible, in fact. For if this woman *has* been carrying around disease, we don't know where she is. And an even bigger question stands: How is she *able* to carry typhoid if she's never *had* typhoid?

We reached the next home, where the lady remembered Mary, and the sickness. There, a girl of eighteen had *died* from the fever. The sadness of that muted me, a girl nearly my age succumbing.

The following day we continued down the list, and each time, yes, they caught the fever, and the cook nursed them, or left shortly after. Of the nine households we visited last week, six suffered from typhoid fever during the time Mary cooked for them. At the other three homes, no one answered our call.

All totaled: Twenty-seven ill, one dead. And these are only the families we know about.

By the end of the week, Mr. Soper appeared struck as if hit by a physical blow. It was quite obviously painful for him to have his revolutionary idea confirmed. I could think of no way to console him, nor could I ease my own heartsickness.

Once we spoke to the last family, my chief sat me down in our office and explained the new scientific theory that was fueling our search. Dr. Koch, a scientist in Germany, has put forth this idea: That a healthy person can carry disease inside himself without suffering from it, and can transmit this disease without knowing it, a so-called healthy carrier. This is a theory I simply cannot understand. If it's true, then how did Mary get the disease inside her in the first place? Why doesn't she become ill herself? How come the sickness doesn't go away like it normally would once it has run its course?

This news, this trail of fevered and dead, has left me sore inside, and deeply sad.

The challenge ahead of us is to find this elusive cook and test her for the typhoid germ by examining her body fluids. Mr. Soper has charged me with telephoning all the employment bureaus in the city next week, not giving up until I find her.

November 30, 1906

Crossing Cherry Park yesterday, I encountered a sick dog expelling from its body wormlike creatures—it was particularly offensive, but I found myself drawn to watching the worms move about on the ground after dog and owner left. I wondered at my own fascination, and the lowly act of observing excrement in the dirt. I thought what I might do if one of my schoolmates were to see me, or worse yet, Mrs. Browning. But a stronger thought overwhelmed me, an understanding that was too powerful to turn away from.

It was this: The worms showed me Mr. Soper's scientific theory.

They showed me how one creature can live inside another, eating from it. Once sated, the creature is expelled out into the world through the feces, where another animal can pick it up. It became clear to me how the fever spreads—if the cook uses the toilet while she is working and doesn't clean her hands well before returning to the kitchen, she passes the typhoid creature—bacteria, he called it—out of her body and into her household's. Mr. Soper has told me that these germs are shaped like noodles, and maybe they have limbs to propel them. Fascinating how living things can live inside us. But I still don't see why Mary doesn't get sick herself.

I must figure that part out, if I can.

I wish I could get into the laboratory and look through the microscope and see for myself what this typhoid germ looks like, but Mr. Soper has not yet responded to my few subtle queries to that effect. In fact, he had me working all week at the task of contacting every employment bureau in the city by telephone to find Mary Mallon.

I have never used a telephone and I was quite excited at first; I had the impression a voice would magically appear at the other end like in a conversation. Instead, it required heavy manual labor to produce a reply. You have to crank the handle on the square wooden box to speak to the switchboard operator, and that handset—like holding an iron against my ear! Half the bosses I reached seemed to be answering from beneath the river, the other half had tin throats. Most times,

They call it talking by lightning.

I had to yell and repeat my query, and pressed the set so close to my ear for replies, I feel as if I've been pummeled. I studied the instrument, the box, the wires, the metal handset, and still cannot figure out how a voice can travel through it all. Mr. Soper says the telephone converts the voice into electrical impulses, which vibrate the wire and then are transformed back into what sounds like a voice. It has to do with the characteristics of sound waves. An invention of affection, he called it—Mr. Bell created the telephone to communicate with his mother and his wife, who were both deaf.

By the end of the week, I was almost wishing I had one of the convenient contraptions at home, imagining Anushka had one too. The wonder of it was, finally, that I could locate the cook's present employment bureau, and all without taking

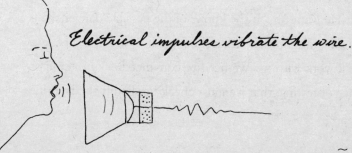

Electrical impulses vibrate the wire.

a single streetcar trip. From the bureau, we found out that the cook currently works for a family on Fifth Avenue. Mr. Soper spent some time thinking of how to approach her.

"I imagine she must be wondering why it is that the typhoid follows her to each job," he said.

"I think she'd be grateful to know that she carries the disease inside her and spreads it like a spice in her cooking," I said.

Of course, I did not mean it to be a joke, it was simply the picture that came to me, but Mr. Soper's brow darkened at my words, and he barked at me sharply, "Prudence, this is an epidemic we're facing here. This woman is very likely responsible for a girl's death, and the illness of many others, and a humorous approach will not help her fathom the gravity of the situation. We must find a way to explain this in the proper manner to her, in a way she'll understand."

His admonishment still rings in my head. I apologized, but Mr. Soper hardly heard me. My foolishness hung from me like a sign.

He went on, "If she knows of the possible danger she is bringing into households, if she is made aware of it, I believe she'll work with us. We need to convince her of the importance of testing, that we must check her bodily fluids, urine, blood, and feces. We must tread lightly with her, however, *as this is a new theory, and not yet proven.*"

"Surely she'll understand that she's connected somehow," I ventured to him, trying to make up for my joke.

"We'll approach her at her place of work," he said. "The laboratory results will give us our answer."

He turned his attention to another task in the office, and I watched him for a minute over my typewriter. Here is a man who has not only solved epidemics, but other things too, like the running water they installed in our neighborhood tenements, and the toilets they put downstairs—all of this to conquer those things that cause death. His goal is cleanliness, an orderliness that will bring health to everyone who lives here. I feel sometimes as if I'm drowning in a sea of unknowns and Mr. Soper is like a ship passing. I call to him, but my mouth is full of dark water, and soon he is out of reach. He seems to work all hours, and never speaks of a family he must return to, not even for holidays like Thanksgiving. He is the first person I've met whose home life I cannot imagine. He never seems to need a rest; he lives for his work. One day I hope to be like him, my whole soul focused on my work, to the exclusion of all else.

Yet I think I would be lonely without my family. We

spent the holiday with Aunt Rachel and Uncle David in Williamsburg, and they were so generous, baking pumpkin pie and turkey legs, mashed yam and challah bread to celebrate the coming together of the Pilgrims and the red man. Uncle David invited a man from the factory, and I'm not sure how to feel about him. Directly after supper Marm sat alone, apple-cheeked in the corner, until the man went over and presented himself to her. It seemed expected that the two of them would meet, this man and Marm (I believe Uncle David invited him for that purpose) and I watched Marm very closely for her reaction. It's been eight years since my father left, and in all that time, men's attentions have rolled off my pretty Marm like water drops. I think my absence and the emptiness of my long work hours away from our apartment has given her thought. Maybe she is worried I'll leave her, maybe the day has come—maybe my matchmaking aunt, as she has tried in the past, has succeeded in convincing her it's time.

The thought hardens my stomach. This man from Uncle David's factory is handsome, with rounded features and a streak of gray in his otherwise dark hair. His eyes look directly and intelligently at a person. Despite Marm's discomfort, he was impressively persistent and discussed all manner of subjects with her. But Marm is not like her sister Rachel, comfortable in her marriage to the same man for twenty-two years. She, like me, is used to being alone.

A peachy glow rose on her cheeks as they spoke, and she laughed at the things he said. Her eyes flitted to me, seeming surprised at her own laughter, guilty at it even, yet she seemed engaged, happy, joyous in a way I haven't seen her in a long time. I have to say, it bothered me. I loved to see her so happy, but I worried about my father, what he might think, what our neighbors would say, Marm with another man—yet even Mrs. Zanberger thinks Marm should surrender the thought of my father's return. . . .

Before the night was through, the man was able to extract a promise of an outing with Marm.

I cannot imagine her on an outing with a man. It doesn't fit. She is otherwise occupied, she is married, she's mated for life until death. . . .

Later I overheard Aunt Rachel and Uncle David talking in the kitchen about Marm marrying this man, and that made my throat hurt. What if the day came and my father returned and Marm had married Mr. Silver? What would happen to my father? What would happen to me?

I feel torn by this man's appearance—concerned for my lonely Marm and fearful of my father's broken heart, should he ever return. I feel we should wait for him, just me and Marm alone, even if that means waiting forever. Receiving his checks is a reminder of him every month; it keeps alive the hope that he will come back, despite what our neighbors and friends say.

I talked with Marm about the man on the way home, and she seemed to view him kindly.

"He is a friend, Prudence, a gentle person to talk to, one who knows your aunt and uncle, that's all."

"He seemed keen on you," I said.

She pulled me to her and kissed my cheek. We held hands. She said, "I know what you're thinking, and there's nothing to worry about. He knows about—your father. And he mentions only friendship."

"That's all?" I asked.

"That's all," she said.

I worry that my Marm contains pockets of loneliness that even a daughter cannot fill.

When I think about my father, I feel as if he and I are in a dense fog. He's backing away from me slowly, the edges of the fog closing in on him, making it harder and harder for me to see him. Any day, I fear, any day he'll turn away from me and be gone from my sight forever.

December 7, 1906

I have not been able to rid my mind of the look on that woman's face—a wide-eyed dread at first, then a closing, smaller, as if her features were swelling shut, the anger turning her freckles a deep brown, spotting her high forehead. The fear, what is it from? I cannot figure out this cook, I cannot figure out this case; it seems to be getting more confusing to me the further we proceed.

Monday morning, cautious and grave, Mr. Soper and I took the elevated train up Sixth Avenue to 57th Street and marched our way to Central Park and over to Fifth Avenue, up to the mansion where Mary Mallon works. We rang the bell and said we were from the Department of Health and Sanitation. We know now not to mention our real purpose until we speak to the head of the household. The very pleasant butler showed us to a dazzling parlor, where he asked us to wait while he fetched his employer. But his kindness gave me an eerie feeling; he seemed to be expecting us. Mr. Soper briefly met my eyes in question as we waited.

I couldn't help admiring the polished shine of the furniture and the floors and the window glass. I wondered how disease might come to such immaculate homes. How did it manage to survive in places with maids who swept and scrubbed daily? It was easy to see it in my own building, where we all live so close together and can practically feel each other's coughs through the walls. But in a large, sparkling house with so few people—how did the bacteria continue to live?

The butler returned and said his employer would be down shortly, as soon as he finished tending to his wife.

Mr. Soper asked what ailed the wife.

The butler seemed bewildered. "Didn't you state you were from the Department of Health?" he asked. He thought we had been summoned by his employer.

"We are in fact investigating a typhoid epidemic," Mr. Soper answered.

"Typhoid, yes!" the butler exclaimed. "The same disease that has felled the missus. Their daughter was hospitalized with it last night."

A gasp slipped from me; it was unprofessional, but I couldn't help it.

At that moment, the man of the house came into the parlor and sank to the sofa; he was dressed in night shoes and gown. He rested his forehead in his hands and sighed. "I'm so glad you're here."

Mr. Soper sat across from him and said, "My assistant and I were engaged to hunt down the source of a typhoid epidemic that probably began some years ago."

"The vomiting started after we took Melissa to the hospital," the man said.

"I'm sorry," Mr. Soper said. "I must be clear, I'm not a medical doctor."

The man looked up and Mr. Soper went on, "I'm investigating this epidemic. Our findings have led us here. I believe you've hired a cook named Mary Mallon. We have reason to think she has unwittingly brought the disease to you."

"My cook is not ill," the man said. "She never has been."

"I understand," Mr. Soper said. "We believe she doesn't need to be ill to carry the typhoid."

"I've never heard of such a thing," the man said.

"We only ask that she submit to testing at our offices," Mr. Soper said.

"But her bureau says the only sickness she's ever had was the common cold," the man said.

Maybe he was distracted by his worry, but the man was very resistant to the idea that his cook carried the typhoid disease. Mr. Soper insisted—we must have the chance to test her; it's the only way to rule her out.

"I think you're wasting your time, but if you say you can prevent the spread of the disease . . . ," the man said. He showed us to the kitchen and introduced us to a tall, flame-haired woman with a knife in her hand and a half-cut onion on the chopping block before her. This was Mary. I could not stop myself from staring at her. In my mind, I had pictured a Medusa, a pox-ridden hag with missing teeth and long, dirty fingernails crawling with worms, yet standing before us was a woman who looked proper and stately, hair in a bun, apron neatly ironed, nails trim and pink.

Mr. Soper started by telling her we were from the Department of Health and Sanitation of the City of New York, and she resumed slicing her onion.

"My kitchen is clean," she said.

There was not a mark on her skin. Even her collar was starched and brilliant white.

"With all respect, Miss Mallon, we have reason to believe

you may be involved in the carriage of typhoid without your knowing it," Mr. Soper said.

"What do you mean, I'm involved?" she said. She spoke in a thick Irish brogue. "I ain't been sick a day in me life!"

I don't mean to poke fun at her accent by writing it this way; I simply want to test the degree to which I can accurately relate these details.

Mr. Soper asked her to think back over her work history.

"I worked for a dozen loverly families," she said. "What about 'em?"

"The disease seems to follow you, doesn't it?" Mr. Soper asked. "Wouldn't you like to know why that is?"

She glanced quickly at her employer, who seemed impatient and upset.

"Aye, I know why 'tis," she said. "This city's full of sickness—everywhere you look, there's people droppin' with the typhoid and the croup. 'Tain't no surprise, mister, people get sick all the time."

Mr. Soper persisted, "Yes, but the typhoid in particular seems to follow you, ma'am. If one is not careful, disease can enter the food one prepares. Especially raw, uncooked food like peach ice cream."

The woman stopped slicing and looked up.

Her employer interjected here: "Mary is a cleanly person and a fine cook. Of course she washes—I wouldn't hire anyone who wasn't completely scrupulous in every way. This is a waste of time! I must get back to my wife! Please, let me show you to the door."

Mr. Soper didn't move.

Oniony tears watered Mary's eyes. She squinted them away and said to Mr. Soper in a bitter voice, "You saying I ain't clean?"

"We could solve this issue if you'd simply come to my office and give a sample of your fluids," Mr. Soper said. His voice softened as he got more frustrated with these stubborn people.

"My what?" the cook asked just as quietly.

"Your fluids," he repeated.

"What in the world—," she started to protest, and my chief interrupted.

"Your fluids, such as your blood, for example, will tell us if you carry disease."

"You want blood?" she screeched, scaring the life out of me. I feared she had completely lost her mind, shouting that way in front of the master of the house.

"Mary, please!" her employer said.

Mr. Soper said, "Your blood, yes."

She took the knife in her hand and stabbed it into the chopping block with a high-pitched yell. "I'll give you blood!"

Her employer turned to us. "Mr. Soper, why don't you find the real reason for this typhoid, for God's sake, instead of upsetting my staff!"

Mary struggled to remove the knife.

The man waved his arms at us. "Please, I'll have to ask you to leave. I have enough problems without your wild accusations."

"But all I ask is for one small sample."

"If you don't leave, I'll have to complain to the department!"

Mary hollered, "Get out of here! Out! Out with your foul ideas! Go on!"

Her eyes rolled up, I could see the whites of them, and her teeth.

"Please, ma'am, it is very important that we test you—"

She screeched and yanked the knife out of the block and started coming around; Mr. Soper turned on his heel, scooting me out of that house in front of him. And that was the last we spoke to her.

A disaster. Not at all what we imagined, this woman. Not

in the least. The incident disturbed Mr. Soper profoundly. It has put a brick wall in our way. All week he muttered to himself that we must get to her, we must explain to her so she'll understand. I watch him sifting through the records, repeating to himself that we must figure a way to have her tested, or she will continue spreading the fever, and someone else will die. Maybe even that girl in the hospital. He pinches the bridge of his nose and says we must stop her.

Short of kidnapping, I don't know how he will get to her. But we must figure out a way. Mr. Soper tried patiently to explain the problem to her, but she responded so very badly. Why won't she cooperate with us? Does she honestly not believe Mr. Soper, despite the evidence that the disease follows her?

He says he can see in her eyes that she fears for her job, and that is the only thing that makes sense to me.

December 14, 1906

In pondering Mary Mallon's response, I think that Mr. Soper's accusation in front of her employer must've given her a great surprise and embarrassment. But I don't think we were wrong. We simply asked her for a test of her fluids. I'm beginning to see that people in the sciences often have to think in a different realm, somewhere beyond human emotions. They must hold their feelings in a dark cave deep inside themselves and never release them. They can't be afraid of embarrassment, neither in themselves, nor others.

Yet I think it must be tremendously difficult to accept that you have a thing living in you, a disease that you can't see, or taste, or touch. One that doesn't make you ill. Perhaps it's too frightening for her to contemplate. It's not like lice you can just pluck off your skin, or a rash you can heal with cream. And it's never been proven. But this cook, if she has any sense, *must* suspect that Mr. Soper's accusation is right.

However, as far as we know, she has not left her place of work, so perhaps she thinks his theory is complete poppycock.

The cook's reaction has given Mr. Soper pause. She is a rarity—a new discovery, really, very possible living proof of Dr. Koch's theory, the first of her kind, and Mr. Soper does not want to frighten her off. He also doesn't want her to continue working and possibly spreading the disease, so we have a special situation on our hands. I believe Mr. Soper is contemplating bringing in our superintendent, Mr. Briggs, but I don't think he is ready for that step yet. Mr. Soper says we must prove to her the danger she carries, and then this epidemic will stop.

He says we must approach the cook as if she were a rabid animal. We must corner her with care and tact, draw her in for testing. Mr. Soper is thinking of trailing her to her home, where we can talk with her in some measure of privacy. We can't approach her at the mansion again, and we don't want to alert her bureau by inquiring about her further.

I'm not sure how I feel about trailing after her. Are we really to follow her like spies? I don't remember reading any examples of this kind of detective work in my chief's records. But I must rely on Mr. Soper as my guide; he knows what is best.

December 16, 1906

This case is so important to me, I hate to leave in the middle, but I'm simply aching to see my dearest friend and talk to her. We've been planning this trip for nearly a year, and I decided I'll go mad if I don't see my Anushka soon, so I booked the ticket to Virginia from the twenty-fourth to the twenty-seventh with the Southern Line. Four days was all the holiday Mr. Briggs would give, and he did not do so willingly. I paid for the ticket with my own funds, which made me feel a bona fide member of the adult world.

When I imagine myself alone on a huge locomotive all the way to Virginia, I feel small and scared as a young child. When I think of traveling out of New York for the first time in my whole life, I feel big as a grown woman. Will Anushka be happy to see me after all this time? What gifts can I take along that will remind her of our crowded city life and what she left behind? Perhaps I could bring a bottle of backfire from the motor carriages. A song from the hurdy-gurdy player? Or I could gather up the neighbors and pay Mr. Barnical two whole dollars for a photograph of all of us in front of her old tenement building. I can see Anushka looking at it, pointing out Mrs. Zanberger and the Moscowitz boys, and both of us bursting into those great gales of wonderful, loud laughter that I can feel all the way down to my toes.

I was, for a time, worried about leaving Marm as I have never done so before, and she has had enough loved ones leave her, but her first outing with her new friend Mr. Silver went so well, I think maybe she'll survive without me. Mr. Silver took her to the Metropolitan Museum, and Marm arrived home full of stories and a smile that wouldn't leave her eyes. It seems Mr. Silver has frequented the museum with paper and pencil, and spends time copying the pictures and figures, and knows the history of the masterpieces, and the Greek and Italian artifacts, and told Marm all about them. I'd be curious to see how good those drawings really are.

When I return from my trip, the three of us together will attend the New Year's celebration over at the factory near Herald Square where Mr. Silver is a cutter, and Uncle David tailors. They will be frying fish in barrels of oil on the street, and setting off firecrackers, and dancing to an oompah band. This party will give me a chance to become better acquainted with Mr. Silver. It will give me the opportunity to thank him for his kindness to my lonely Marm, and to remind him of my father's existence, which he, like us, must never forget for a moment.

December 20, 1906

I had a strange and illuminating conversation with my chief while waiting in the freezing weather outside of the Fifth Avenue home where Mary Mallon works. It was our second attempt at trailing her, but she had not come out of the mansion, and I felt somehow it was below Mr. Soper's dignity to stand out in the cold for naught, so I said, "It's rather brisk for such a task, don't you think, sir?"

His gaze on the house was quite intense, as if he could make her appear with his eyes.

"I've been through far, far worse," he said.

"I imagine you have," I said. "You lived through a war."

A nervous pinch started in my stomach; I wasn't sure why I had brought up the war. Maybe the cold had numbed my fear, or maybe I thought, there in the dark, that it might be a good time to dare a question about my father.

"The war, yes," he said. "We spent long days trying to find out what made those men so ill."

"Did you know any of the—the soldiers—personally?" I asked.

I was hoping he might connect my father's name with mine and miraculously recall the short, curly-haired, olive-skinned man who belonged to me.

"It was not a time of socializing," Mr. Soper said. He blew his breath onto his hands to keep warm. "I was too busy with research and observation to really get to know the men," he said.

A stab of disappointment let the air from me. We stood in silence, our eyes on the mansion.

"It's interesting when you think of war, how bacteria can also be used as a weapon," Mr. Soper said suddenly.

"What do you mean?" I asked.

"Well, for instance, during the Civil War, men from the South would send men from the North blankets."

"A gesture of truce?" I asked, not understanding.

"Quite the opposite," he said. "The blankets had been wrapped around men who died of smallpox. They would spread the deadly disease to their enemies through those blankets."

This story shook me—it made me angry to think of disease, and bacteria, and how dangerous those tiny organisms were to us.

"Mr. Soper," I said, "I think I would understand this case much better if I could see, actually see what the typhoid bacteria looks like."

I watched, even in the darkness, the muscles twitching in his jaw.

I dared to add, "Through the microscope, I mean."

"Perhaps," he said, "perhaps it would be a good idea for you to see them. Then you'd understand better how they pass from person to person."

A rush of blood flowed through me. He agreed to allow me to look in the microscope! First thing tomorrow morning, I will see, I will put my eye to that bronzed lens and see what this world is made of! I shiver with anticipation, with the promise of our undertaking. I can hardly sleep, imagining what it might be like to look at real bacteria. The things I will understand, the doors that will open to me! Oh, I cannot wait!

December 21, 1906

Bright and early this morning, we went into the laboratory (not before the science fellows arrived— I could feel every cool, male eye on me). Mr. Soper took a typhoid sample from the icebox and swabbed it on a slide and slipped it into a free scope.

Once I looked into the microscope, my idea about cells and bacteria transformed. In my mind, they had always been as inert as drawings.

Here, they were alive. Like tiny worms, dozens of them.

Before me, these restless creatures wriggled their way around the slide. They were nearly see-through, as if they were made of water. They danced and moved just like a crowd in the street, gathering and separating in their own way. Like little noodles one might swallow so easily, without knowing. I felt as if I were seeing the river's floor, or another country, places earlier off-limits to me. It astonished and dismayed me, that those minuscule bacteria had the force to kill a person.

My eye to the microscope made me want to see more, to see deeper into the world.

I want to see a nerve cell. A sample of blood. The leaf of a plant, my fingernail, a piece of hair. I want to take the instrument home and slide the world under my lens, to examine it in a way I never have before.

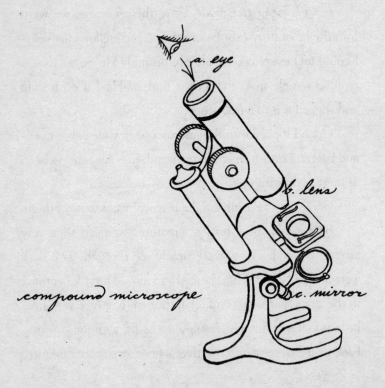

a. eye

b. lens

compound microscope   *c. mirror*

December 23, 1906

In thinking over the typhoid bacteria I saw in the microscope, I think perhaps our cook is made of something that isn't quite human, that doesn't respond to these tiny sickening cells. It's almost as sinister as Mary Shelley's Frankenstein, this idea. Maybe that's why our cook doesn't want to come in for testing. She doesn't get sick and won't admit that she makes other people sick—she can't see what we're talking about at all.

I wish we could bring the microscope to her and show her what typhoid looks like. I wish we didn't have to stake her out like a criminal. Or corner her like an animal. It doesn't feel quite right to approach her this way.

I must trust that Mr. Soper knows what he is doing by trailing her. We still have not seen her come out of the mansion.

I think it'll be a relief to have a few days away from this case. We've been working with such focus, I simply cannot see clearly. Just three more days, and I'll be on my way to Anushka. I'm nervous about the trip, but I'm glad to go—I can't wait to see my best friend's smiling face.

I fear Mr. Soper will be spending the holiday alone—he speaks only of work, of Mary Mallon, and how to get her to submit to testing. When I asked him about his plans for Christmas, he shrugged my question away. From the notes, I can see he's been working late and on Sundays, trying to figure out if his theory is wrong in any way, if there is something we missed, some other way these families could've fallen ill. I believe he does not wish to encounter the woman's kitchen knife again if he doesn't have to. I think the incident embarrassed him as well as Mary, and we need to contact her more successfully next time.

There is so much to think over, so many things I don't know. I see Mr. Soper working on this case in my absence—what will he do if he has to face that cook alone? While I hope he does find her residence, I pray that no harm comes to him while I am gone.

December 28, 1906

I hardly know where to begin writing my impressions of Anushka's farm and the trip. It was such a whirlwind, I have not yet caught my breath nor collected my thoughts into any sort of coherent line. I did not realize how far Virginia was, nor the many different lands I'd be passing through. I arrived home yesterday, this morning, actually, after nearly ten hours in that bumpy, rocking locomotive, and still I feel the ground moving beneath me.

Tired as I am, I have to write, even a quick entry; there is so much I must record. To a large degree, the trip was nothing like what I expected. The amount of acreage her father owns—how striking that he was able to save enough money from the bookshop to buy such a piece of land. I keep thinking of the grandness of the farm, the distance I could see, endless ground covered in a white shawl of snow. I felt my eyes stretching, looking for miles ahead of me to the horizon where earth meets sky. I have never looked so far in my life.

The house struck me so. It looked raw—walls and floors of big planks whitewashed clean, the railwood furniture, knots and grains left intact, the row of butter churns, the cast-iron range, big enough to feed the boys and all of their friends, and hers. Her parents busy, but with work that made them whistle. The warmth of the woodstove in the living room. The walk we took in the woods, the way we scared rabbits from their holes, and partridges—no, pea hens, she called them—and all of her beautiful animals, horses, lambs, chickens. I didn't realize the extent of her responsibilities, how much labor is involved in running a farm. And this not even planting season! Every moment is taken up—the feeding, cleaning, grooming, slaughtering, smoking, shoveling— I was awed by the muscles in her arms!

I have never tasted lamb so fresh; next to the herring I brought, the chops seemed to be practically walking. The potato pancakes her mother made, the onions her father jarred, the bread and honey—goodness, I think I have gained ten pounds in three days.

On my second afternoon with her, when we had finished

all her chores (I accompanied her, but was not obliged to work nearly as hard as her), Anushka took me to a nearby pond that had frozen over. She wouldn't say why—she still has that impish sense of mystery. When we got to the edge, suddenly she cried out, "Watch!" and ran onto the ice. Right before my eyes, she flopped onto her bottom and slid across the entire expanse of the pond, petticoats flying, bloomers exposed to the birds!

A shock of cold air caught in my throat, then I exploded into a great burst of laughter—I couldn't help it—she looked so very silly and daring at the same time. She ran over the ice back to me, her curls bouncing, her breath coming in heavy white puffs, and she dragged me out onto that pond with her. There was nobody else for miles around. We slipped and fell and skittered all around the frozen water until the day darkened. I have not laughed so much for nearly a year. It felt as if we had not skipped a single day in our togetherness, but rather picked up right where we had left each other.

But time *is* changing us, pulling us deeper into life without having each other to turn to. I felt like she needed me, but I couldn't pinpoint how or why. It was on the last day, when I met her friends Ida and Randall, and saw Anushka's relation to them, that I understood how she holds her darker feelings inside now, how she guards them from me almost.

In her letters, and before we met them, Anushka didn't tell me of her friends' advanced ages. Ida is twenty-seven, Randall a man of thirty, which is nearly Mr. Soper's age. It was clear how she could love both those people—our conversation with them ranged far and wide. They were both so full of knowledge about the natural world, the way they named trees and celestial bodies, Randall's reading of clouds, Ida's firm way with the animals, they were both so easy with themselves, and each other. Randall's power and skill, his long, sensitive face and thick blond hair, are very alluring. I understand how Anushka could have a terrible mash on him. Ida's quick smile, and the deep way she listens when one speaks, has great charm as well. Their backgrounds are so different—Randall from wealthy Protestant stock, Ida a second-generational transplant from Lutheran Germany, and Anushka, the New York Russian Jew—but it was a sweet camaraderie.

Yet here is the difficulty: Those two friends of hers are in love with each other.

It's clear how impossible it's been for Anushka to state her feelings, to choose, as I'd been urging her. Randall is kind to her. Ida's too wonderful to lose. But they have chosen each other. The pain Anushka must feel, my poor friend, the tear of the heart.

I do hope Anushka finds another beau, someone who can see how very darling she is.

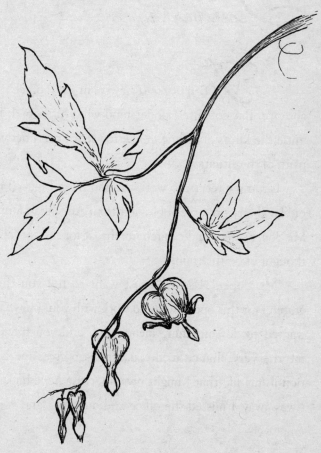

December 29, 1906

Things went awry in the office in my absence. I'm not sure I understand what happened. I must untie the knots of feeling in me, to see if I can uncover the truth of the situation.

Upon my return to work this morning, I placed the jar of blackberry preserves I brought from Anushka's farm onto Mr. Soper's desk and cleared my throat for the speech I had thought of on the train.

"Mr. Soper," I said, "I just want to tell you that I'm grateful for this opportunity to work with you. I have always wanted to do something meaningful, and you have given me the very chance to do so. This job gives me a direction in my life that I might not otherwise have had. While I was away, I missed the office and our work and you—my employer—"

There my words faltered; the way Mr. Soper averted his gaze made me feel uncouth. My gift and admission seemed to affect my chief oddly—he said, "Hm, yes, well, thank you, but you weren't gone so long. I've spent many years alone." He grabbed some notes and began to read, completely dismissing me and my speech.

I sat at my typewriter, my face aflame. I excused myself and headed for the lavatory, where I splashed a bit of water on my cheeks and loosened my shirtwaist at the neck.

When I returned, I began to type up the notes from the days I had missed. They were few, and simple. I saw that Mr. Soper had not gotten very much further with the case.

Later in the day, Mr. Soper straightened his cuffs and began to put on his jacket as if he were about to leave the office. He said, without meeting my eyes, "I think I have found a person who could show me where Mary Mallon lives."

I had not seen this in his notes—such an important occurrence!

Still not looking at me, he said, "I caught sight of Mary while you were gone. She visited a place I want to return to this afternoon."

I stood from my desk and quickly gathered up pencils and folio.

"Prudence, I want you to stay here, in the office, to catch up on work you missed," he said.

I felt him strange and distant.

"Sir, I've finished most of my work and would have no trouble coming with you."

He seemed to look at me as though he were evaluating my character.

He sighed and tapped his desk. "You may come," he said. "But leave the folio in the office. I don't want to be obvious."

We took a trolley north to 33rd Street, where we exited and walked east. My chief stopped just outside a saloon— a beat-up front called Donovan's with spittoons on the side-walk, dank gaslights, and loud laughter and music emanating from its doors. Something about the place frightened me; I looked to Mr. Soper for explanation. He glanced at me— then he took a breath and said, "You're to stay close to me at all times, Prudence. Don't touch anything, don't speak to anyone, just stay near. Do you understand?"

I swallowed the grip of fear in my throat, and we went in. The stink of coal hit me, and the smell of food—sausage, pickle, sauerkraut, stew. On top of it all, the odor of bodies nearly made me choke. Every table was filled, a lunch crowd of gamblers and streetwalkers shoveling kraut and links from hot bins into their plates, swigging from steins of brew. The clamor bewildered me. I recognized faces—cigar-smoking Officer O'Malley, for one, and Mr. Jackson, the smithy, drunkards both. The rest looked stale and ravenous, hedonist, with garish mouths and careless ways, a group as bad as those who hang out at the Poor Man's Retreat—old Five Points gang members now gone decrepit. With their ill-gotten money, they're worse than any of our neighborhood bums. I wished I had not agreed to go, but I wanted to find out our purpose. I held my breath and steadied myself with my hand on Mr. Soper's arm as he led me through that boisterous crowd.

He stopped at a table in the very back where sat an unshaven man with rummy eyes. The rummy looked at Mr. Soper and nodded. I moved behind my chief, fearful of the man, yet curious, as Mr. Soper seemed to know him.

My chief put several dollars on the table.

"Did you set up the meeting with Mary Mallon?" he asked.

A sick feeling sank in my stomach.

The dirty rummy slid the dollars off the table. "Aye," he said.

A bribe! I had just watched my chief bribe a man.

I couldn't see Mr. Soper's face, but his shoulders curved

down, his head low to the table. For a moment, he didn't seem any different from the bums around him.

I looked left and right. What was I doing in this dank place? What were *we* doing there? Why had our search for Mary come to this? It was wrong, it was improper. It was immoral. I wanted to push the scene away, to deny that it was my honorable chief making such a lowly offering to such a dirty man, but there he was.

"Mary's comin' home Wednesday night," the rummy snarled.

Mr. Soper set out another few dollars. "When should we come by?" he asked.

"Aye, we'll set it up for eight, we'd be eatin' around eight."

That man took the bills and sold out his girl, just like a piece of chicken.

I followed Mr. Soper out of that saloon, all the way back to our office, and I could think of nothing to say. He did not offer an explanation; he did not even look at me. My mind rapidly tried to make up excuses for him, but none seemed right. What he had done was simply beyond my comprehension! Suddenly he seemed unpredictable to me, even questionable. A stranger. He had acted alone in the time I'd been gone—while making no notes in our common folio.

I feel I don't know what happened in our office while I was away. I wonder if Mr. Soper has done this sort of thing before and has not kept record of it—to protect himself? To hide?

How can I work in an office with a man who does such things? How can I trust that he will not lead me astray in some way?

I wish I could speak to Marm about this, but the act has so shamed me, I could not possibly do so. She would surely be upset.

She might even want me to leave the job.

December 31, 1906

On this last night of the year, as I wait for Marm to return so we can attend the festivities, I feel as if a whole different girl is trying to emerge from me. Like I'm about to visit one of those cocoon tea parties, cloaked in dull gray. Inside, I will reveal a silver and pink gown, and win the prize as the most beautiful butterfly.

At work this evening, I watched Mr. Soper prepare for the planned meeting with Mary Mallon at her home. The lines on his face seemed deeply engraved, his darting eyes would not meet mine. We had not spoken about the incident with the rummy. I knew I could go with him, that Marm would not be waiting for me, but I expected he didn't want me to accompany him to Mary's home. As I watched him dress in wool overcoat and leather gloves, I thought of the rummy's wicked face, and Mary Mallon with her knife raised, and it struck me: These are frightening people—foreign, dangerous even. If Mr. Soper went alone, something might happen to him, and no one would know about it. I felt my responsibility then. I stood; I didn't want to see him hurt, despite my reservations about him.

When I threw my cape over my shoulders and gathered my folio, he put up his hand to stop me.

"I will speak to Mary alone," he said.

"Please, Mr. Soper, I believe I can be useful."

"Not tonight, Prudence, I must go myself."

"I'll wait outside then, in case there's an emergency," I said. He paused.

"She seems to be such an unpredictable woman, sir."

I worried he'd continue the case without me, but I was convinced my presence might help him to stay a proper course. I wanted to make sure Mary would agree to come peacefully this time. I didn't like the misgivings I held toward my chief, but I wanted things to go well, for us to get some long-awaited answers.

He put on his bowler without further discussion, and I followed him out the door.

We made our way to the dark address the rummy had given us. Neither his name nor Mary's were on the downstairs door of this ratty place, an uneven-floored tenement, worse than anything on our street, four stories of dirty tiles, print-smeared walls, halls barely lit. We went upstairs and pounded on 4D, as the rummy said, but only a dog answered with yip and howl. Mr. Soper banged and rapped, raising up a ruckus of furious barking, and finally the neighbor's door cracked open and a voice snarled, "Hang it up! They ain't home, they gone till Monday!" and the door snapped shut.

We both stared at it. I couldn't help but wonder at the inch of relief I felt.

"It's a circus!" Mr. Soper exclaimed. "This is the worst kind of human circus. I cannot believe, I simply cannot believe our luck with this woman!"

On the trolley downtown, he ground his fist into his bowler and muttered about making unsuccessful contracts with questionable people.

I could feel his anger like hot rays emanating from him. He bent the rim of his hat between his gloved hands. I glanced over and saw the muscles in his jaw twitching furiously. He sighed heavily through his nose.

We got off the trolley and he walked me to my door as it was late. When we faced each other to bid good night, I could see the pain he held in his eyes.

"This case is becoming—insufferable," he said.

I nodded.

"They—Mary doesn't seem to understand the importance of it," he said.

I shook my head.

"I want nothing more than for her to cooperate—appropriately," he said.

I said, "Mr. Soper, I know that I've not worked for you very long, but I do believe that Mary Mallon is a most impossible person, and that it was very decent of you to try and give her a chance to come in for testing on her own. I know that you *will* find her, and that your theory *will* be proven."

As I spoke, the anger dropped from his eyes. He gave me a most surprising look, one that penetrated through me, through my very cells, almost. It turned something in me, like a key.

"Prudence, your enthusiasm is perfectly contagious," he said. "Continue with the good work."

Before I could reply, he walked quickly to the corner and into the night. I came inside, though I have no appetite for the meal Marm left me. I sit at the table with this new sense, this *feeling*. I think of the timbre of his voice, the gentle way he said my name. I cannot tell what this burning in my chest is. It is sudden, and unexpected, like an Indian summer day, and it contains ribbons of all colors, a rainbow fluttering up through me, shining out of my mouth and eyes, and around my head like a halo.

I am emerging, I'm afraid, like a butterfly, a shimmery bright thing coming into being.

January 1, 1907

A new year. Marm and I went to the festivities at Herald Square last night to celebrate. I stayed long enough to eat a fried pike and crack two fireworks, and to watch Marm's friend Mr. Silver give her a slim shell bracelet. Despite my hesitation, there is something about Mr. Silver's round features that makes me and Marm smile whenever we look at him. I feel myself warming to him, his presence in our lives thawing our hearts.

The streets were crowded with folks dancing and laughing, drinking and singing, their hats falling off, their cheeks red. I polkaed some with Uncle David, which made me feel lonely, that and watching all the lovers kiss at midnight. Marm and I went home shortly after and listened to the fireworks until sleep overtook us.

I will be seventeen this year. I think of my resolutions: to read more books and study more of the sciences on my own. But how? Anushka's father had a treasury of books, those he retained from his store across the street. New science books are far too expensive to buy, and the library contains only musty copies of old textbooks and several difficult medical journals that I have attempted to read in the past, only to feel like I was studying Latin. If it weren't for the illuminating figures, I would understand nothing. Anushka suggested I ask that science fellow to help tutor me, but I'm not sure I wish to have such close relations with him. When by chance I see him in the hallway, he stops me with his eyes and winks. I wait for him to say something, an intelligent scrap that might interest me, but he sees me only as female and can't talk to me any other way, it seems. Very tiring. If only he worked as hard on his mind as he does on his polished appearance.

Anyhow, I know that eventually Mr. Soper can teach me all I need to know.

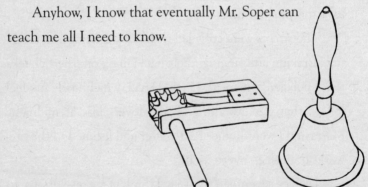

January 5, 1907

We finally contended with the cook again tonight when she arrived home with her rummy. But I was not prepared for how Mr. Soper planned to speak to Mary. His actions confuse and disturb me—I don't know what to think of his behavior.

We watched them pull up in a carriage, get out, and hurry upstairs. Mr. Soper gave them time to settle in, and we proceeded after them. From the hall, we could smell meat frying; the smell got stronger as we ascended, and we could hear the cooking noises coming from their door. Mr. Soper and I exchanged glances—if she's cooking, she may have a weapon handy—but her nearness spurred us on.

He knocked, and stepped back. The dog yipped and scratched his nails on the door. When Mary called out, Mr.

Soper introduced us by name only, and said he simply wished to talk with her for a moment.

The door flew open, and she eyed us. She had a cooking fork in her hand. The little dog pushed his fluffy black head around her legs and growled at us.

"How'd you find me?" was her first question.

Mr. Soper paled; I could see the truth on his tongue, which he didn't want to tell. I felt myself holding my breath.

From inside, the rummy called out, "Who's it, darlin'?" and Mary turned to him, opening the door a little wider. The dog ran out and scratched at our feet, and the rummy saw us and blanched. He called the animal and they disappeared into the apartment, a bit of which I could see, a surprising chaos of rags and dirt, so different from the starched whiteness of her collar.

"Youse followed me here, didn't ye?" Mary said, entering the hall with us and closing the door behind her. She looked straight at me with disgust.

Mr. Soper said he thought she would appreciate speaking to him in the privacy of her own home, rather than at her place of work.

"A sneak, that's what you are," Mary said. "Following me."

The way she tapped the long cooking fork against the door frame gave me a rubbery feeling in my lower half.

"I really honestly do not mean to be sneaky, ma'am," Mr. Soper replied gently. "I just wish to talk to you, to explain to you how important it is to take these tests we spoke of. If you had agreed in the first place—"

"You say I'm dirty—that's all I been hearin' since I got on Ellis Isle—the dirty Irish!" She pointed her fork as she ranted; her anger seemed to gain her a few inches in stature. "Dirty Irish, carryin' disease! Well, I'm sick of it, 'cause it ain't true. I wash me hands, always. I use the freshest goods, I never made anyone sick off me cooking—all's I ever do is nurse those people, and it ain't even my job! If I were so dirty, all of you wouldn't hire me in the first place, so be gone with your diseases and your tests!"

I was ready to leave right then, to find another way to convince her to come into the office, but Mr. Soper didn't give up so easily.

"I'm not accusing you of anything, ma'am," he said, holding up his hand to Mary's fork. "I am a scientific man, and I go only by the sciences. And I believe that it is scientifically proven that a healthy person can possibly carry germs inside them, harmful germs that are invisible to them, but which a test will prove exist. If only you'll come into the office, we can give you a simple test, and you'll be on your way," he said.

"And who's in charge of these tests?" she asked, squinting at both of us in that dim hall.

"Well, the department will administer the test—"

"And they can say anythin' they damn well please, that's right, isn't it?"

"Of course not, Miss Mallon. They'll give an honest testing—"

"I don't see why you're after me, why you won't leave me alone! I never done nothing to nobody, I just want to work, so leave, leave me in peace!" she cried. She was becoming quite agitated, pointing her fork again.

"My God, woman, I have had enough!" Mr. Soper raised his voice at her, and I looked at his blotched face, astonished at the sudden change in him. He shouted, "You have forced me into it! I have a police guard waiting at the ready, and if you don't come with me right now, I will have them take you away like a criminal!"

"Police!" Mary shouted.

"Yes, police! You're sickening people! You are killing people with your cooking and you won't stop. You're a stubborn woman, and you've left me no choice!"

He came right out and accused her. Accused and insulted her. Threatened to have the police arrest her. Were they really downstairs waiting? Was this the way we were to treat her?

"You get the police," she cried, "go on, you nosy bloodsucker. I done nothing wrong." She raised the fork and shouted something I didn't understand, as Mr. Soper turned and pushed me ahead of him. The fork clattered over our heads as we ran down the stairs, and I could hear the crazed woman hollering above.

We reached the street, no policemen there, and Mr. Soper in such an agitation as I've never seen, his eyes unusually animated, his face such a ghostly white that I feared something might be wrong with him. I wondered about all the time he spent alone studying the case. First the bribe, now this lie about a police guard. Was it a lie, or did he have some plan he wasn't telling me? I felt useless, as if I hadn't been doing my job, hadn't been reading his notes. I had missed very important information. I spent the ride home abashed and fuming at myself, and at Mary, and at the confusion I felt again with this case. Mr. Soper had come straight out and called Mary a killer. Her words echoed in my ears—*dirty Irish.*

Is that what Mr. Soper thinks of her?

January 6, 1901

The whole thing has become so bizarre and twisted, I hardly know where I fit in, or what my feelings are. I am shaken, unsure of my own feet on the ground, and that is all I know for certain. Maybe it was my desperation, my need to understand—I don't know—

After arriving home from Mary's, I couldn't sleep. I spent the night watching the moon rise and set, feeling very alone. I had to return to the office, I decided, and look through Mr. Soper's private notes, all the way back to the time when I visited Anushka, even before that, to see what I had missed. It was the only way I would understand Mr. Soper's unpredictable behavior, I thought.

I left a note for Marm and dressed before dawn, just as the first streetcars began running. I hurried through the cold up to 14th Street.

Our office building was unlocked; I thought the cleaners were already at work, and I entered. Instead of turning left toward our office, however, something made me stop. The laboratory. No one would be in there so early. A tickling started inside me, a curiosity as to how the room might appear without all those staring eyes. I turned right and walked to that great laboratory. I could see through the glass door that the globes were lit, but there wasn't a soul inside. I decided to go in, to explore further. I leaned on the first desk and touched the microscope with one finger. I closed my eyes and imagined what it might be like working in that room all day, studying our world from the inside out, and the feeling was glorious. At that moment, I felt so happy, as if I truly understood my purpose in life.

And then I heard someone say, "Looking for me?"

I turned and saw the peculiar science fellow at the other end of the room coming out of a closet, behind him, rows of jars shining like teeth. I stood up straight, caught.

He was holding a bottle of white powder, which he put down. Slowly he started walking toward me, his face wolfishly pointed. I wanted to back up and run away, but the door seemed a mile off, and my legs still as logs.

"What a nice surprise," he said. "You came to see me. I

can't say I was expecting you," he said, all the while advancing on me.

I felt mesmerized by the glittery look in his eyes. My arms tingled—I had never felt frightened of him before, but now, with the building empty, he seemed much bigger than me.

"I know you came in here the other day with Mr. Soper just so you could be near me," he said.

I couldn't believe my ears. "What do you mean?" I asked.

"You weren't interested in seeing no typhoid germs," he said. He sat on the desk close to me. Sitting that way, he overshadowed me like a tree. "You're sweet on me, aren't you?" he said.

His hands seemed ready to touch me. I folded my arms over my chest.

"I—I don't even know you," I said. A strange sensation came over me—I felt sure that if I ran, he'd chase after me.

"Sure you know me," he said.

He was so close, I could smell his gutter mouth. I tried to keep the tremble from my voice as I asked, "Why do you speak to me this way?"

He laughed and slid closer.

"I wouldn't do that," I choked out. I tried not to show my fear—why couldn't I move my feet? Just a few steps back?

"Oh, really? Not even a little kiss?" he asked. "You're so serious all the time. I just want to give you a little kiss to make you smile."

I tried to back away from him, but my legs were frozen. I felt tears stinging my eyes, but I willed myself not to cry. I shook my head.

He leaned in toward me, and I turned my face, holding my breath as I felt his mouth coming near, in my mind, pushing him away—

I heard the door open behind him, and a voice thundered: "What on earth is going on here?"

I opened my eyes and saw with immense relief that it was Mr. Soper. The fellow backed off, immediately pointing to me, saying, "She came in here."

Remembering why I was really there, I felt my mouth open in protest, but no words came out. I could only shake my head, fearful of what the scene might look like.

The fellow said, "I was trying to get some work done, but she interrupted me."

I covered my cheeks with my hands. I couldn't look at Mr. Soper's face; my gaze stuck to my feet.

"Prudence, why are you here so early?" Mr. Soper asked.

I shook my head. I couldn't tell him my plan to look through his private notes.

"You can finish your work later, Jonathan. Get your coat, go see if those samples from the Robertson laboratory are ready. I'll take care of this," Mr. Soper said.

"Thank you, sir," the fellow muttered.

I could feel my hands ball into fists as I watched that boy put on his coat and leave the room. A thin layer of ice covered Mr. Soper's countenance as he closed the door after him.

"I have to say, I am utterly shocked and surprised by your behavior. It is most unbecoming," Mr. Soper said, his face sour as if he'd encountered a wharf rat.

I still couldn't find anything to say.

"Perhaps I made a grave error in hiring you," he said.

"No!" I exclaimed, the word escaping my throat.

"We do not have many women working here, and perhaps there is good reason for that. Their very presence is distracting—but I thought you were different, more advanced than your sex. I see I was wrong," he said.

"Please, no," I said, meeting his eyes. "Mr. Soper, please don't think you were wrong about me. I don't know that boy, I don't care a whit about him."

"What were you doing here, then, Prudence?" he said, his face still tight against me.

I told him about the lights being on, and my awful curiosity. I told him of the boy's attention to me from the very beginning, and his advancement on me. I began to cry; I couldn't help myself. I stood there, covering my wet face with my hands, trying to hide my tears. I wanted to stop crying, to show him that I was no girl, which only made me cry harder.

Mr. Soper took out his handkerchief and came to me, dabbing at my cheeks with awkward movements.

"I'm sorry," I sobbed, "I'm so sorry."

Mr. Soper sighed, and I could feel the rough hair of his coat on my cheek as he reached for me and patted my back.

Near my ear, I heard him say, "It can only bring trouble, one so young and lovely."

I smelled his fragrance, a sweet cologne, and pressed my forehead into the crook of his arm.

He gently extended his arm, pushing me away as he straightened my shoulders. He wiped the last of my tears with his kerchief.

"We will send for a carriage to take you home now, Prudence. You can return tomorrow, when you feel better."

I didn't want to leave him just then, but I could see in

his face that there was no other choice; I put on my hat and told him that the boy lived two blocks from me, that I feared another incident.

He seemed troubled by the mention of the boy, and said he thought that being caught had hopefully embarrassed him sufficiently, and he would most likely bother me no further.

Gently my chief led me to the street by my arm. I felt an ache in my chest. The words he had whispered echoed in my head. Mr. Soper had called me lovely.

The force of my feeling for him overwhelmed me.

As I climbed into the carriage, I looked into his face, wondering if he was feeling the same about me, but a paternal worry had settled over him, and I felt him untouchable. He uttered something about the office, and our work, then paid the driver and sent me off. By the time I arrived home, Marm had already left for the Junger birth.

Here I sit, tangling with this emotional state, trying to wrestle it down. I see that I don't know the first thing about love. It's as if I've taken a poison, one that makes my head dizzy, that gives me an insatiable thirst, not for water, but for the sight of my chief. I try to stand outside myself, to be scientific and unemotional. In order for two people to join, I tell myself, humans have been given this feeling. Does that mean I want to love Mr. Soper? The thought frightens me— I have never even kissed a boy, no less a man. I couldn't possibly want love with him.

I just want to return to work and be near him.

Maybe I should take a sick leave, stay home and talk to Marm about my feeling until it has dissipated. But I think of my old teacher Mrs. Browning's warning then, and know that is impossible.

I could walk the streets all day so the feeling can fly out and disappear into the buildings. But I don't think it will go away so simply.

I don't recognize myself. I don't want to be me. I want a return to my innocence. I *must* have my innocence back, I must *will* it back to me. I have spent a good deal of the day writing out my feelings in a long letter to Anushka, begging her advice.

I wait for tomorrow to begin so I can see him again.

January 7, 1907

At the chime of the churchbells, I dressed, breakfasted with Marm, and left for work.

When I arrived at the office, the first person I saw was the science fellow, who bowed his head with puppy-dog eyes before I could turn away. It seemed to be an apology of sorts, but I didn't feel I could accept it. I entered Mr. Soper's office, but he was not in. I breathed deeply, smelling his cologne, which seemed to course through me like a silvery stream. On my desk, I found a note in his hand which said: *Miss G., In a meeting with Mr. Briggs about M.M. Will return around lunch, Mr. S.*

He had finally given in.

I folded the note carefully and placed it in my desk drawer. I looked for the records of our typhoid case, but Mr. Soper had taken them all to Mr. Briggs for the meeting about

Mary Mallon. There would be no chance for me to re-examine them; even Mr. Soper's private journal was gone. I straightened my desk and looked through my jottings of other cases, distracted every time I heard footsteps or a door slam. Finally Mr. Soper returned.

I looked up from my typing, struck by the handsome curve of his cheek. I saw that the meeting occupied his thoughts, so I asked him about it. He seemed to notice me then and said that Mr. Briggs had listened to the case, that they discussed different options for approaching Mary, and Mr. Briggs would give us his decision soon. He said that they had called the hospital and found out that the little girl who had taken ill had *died*. When they called the mansion, they discovered that Mary had *quit* the family. I stood up and went to his desk.

I felt foolish for my moony feelings about Mr. Soper when this woman, this cook, this very possible *killer* was loose.

"Do you know where she is?" I asked.

He nodded his head slowly. "We called her bureau to inform them of the epidemic, and they said they have assigned her to a new house, the Bowings, a family of six over on the West Side. They were quite rude, in fact. Seems they get a commission for Mary Mallon that they don't want to lose, and they are worried about their reputation. I feel we should warn the family somehow, but it's a risk, and I don't want to scare Mary off again. We must wait for Mr. Briggs to make a recommendation. I have told him that Mary Mallon is a serious danger, and a police guard is in order."

Mr. Soper rubbed his forehead in a way that gave me a glimmer of despair. So he *had* been thinking of calling the police. He went on, "Prudence, I don't want you to come into this building alone ever again, do you understand what I mean?"

I looked at him, the red tinge about his face that comes when he doesn't sleep much.

"Of course, Mr. Soper. I've learned my lesson."

He nodded and handed me a new folio. "Get to work on this until we hear from Mr. Briggs," he said.

I took it and started to type out notes of a new case, but I couldn't put my mind on it. We waited all day to hear from Mr. Briggs, but by this evening, still no word. I won't be able to concentrate on any of our other cases until we hear back from Mr. Briggs about Mary Mallon.

I try to drive away my feelings for my chief, to bury them deep inside the cave of me, but it's not so easy. It *is* like a sickness, this feeling, like a hunger that won't go away. My heart feels like an open wound.

January 14, 1907

The postman brought a reply from Anushka this morning, and in it were the wise words of a truly experienced friend. Her compassion, but more, her directness, entered me like a steel rod. It helped me enormously to read the fact that she made me face: Mr. Soper will never return my affection. To understand that no matter what I do, he will always see me as an office girl, an assistant, even a scientifically-minded person, but never as a woman, helped a great deal. Once I accepted that fact (and cried a bucket of tears), I was able to move on to her three rules of behavior for forbidden love: Keep quiet, keep cool, pretend. I think of her with these rules, the model of manners when in the presence of her Randall—and I remain composed and contained as a corpse.

Mr. Soper is wrapped up in our business with the cook,

especially after hearing from Mr. Briggs. It seems our super-intendent has discussed this case with a number of people, including his colleagues from the fourth floor, where a woman doctor runs the department's center for mothers with infants. This was the first I had heard of such things (the woman doctor *and* the center). The thought of a woman doctor floods me with wonder. I picture a thick, ugly crea-ture who's indelicately pushed her way through a man's field. Questions buzz around me like bees: How did she become a doctor? (I didn't think they allowed women in medical school!) What is it like to be surrounded by male doctors? (As I've learned, some males in the sciences see women as objects of procreation rather than thinking beings.) Would I have a chance to talk with her? Biggest question for me is: Why has Mr. Briggs chosen to discuss this case with her? (I know very well that the problems of mothers with infants is a far cry from our work in epidemiology. How would she know anything about investigating a disease? How would she be useful?)

Mr. Briggs and several department heads gathered for a meeting. It was decided that Dr. Baker (the woman doctor) would be assigned to our case, and once she had read through our records and made a plan with Mr. Soper, she would accompany us, along with a police guard, to the West Side manor where Mary is presently working.

When I heard about the police guard, I felt terrible that the case had reached such a low point. I wished I could talk to the cook alone and beg her to see reason and not respond to us in such a violent way. We are only trying to do good, really; it's awful that she can't comprehend that. I try to picture her life, the strangers who keep approaching her, the trail of fevered she leaves behind, how trapped she must feel. There is no one with whom she can discuss what is happening to her. I can only imagine how she'll respond to this woman doctor, to the team of police, to us once again on her doorstep.

January 18, 1907

Tonight I am to accompany Marm and Mr. Silver to the flickers, which will take my mind off this case for a few blessed hours. I have been in their lighthearted company three times, and he is a gentleman in every sense. He treats Marm with such kindness and generosity, and me as well, that I can feel tendrils of attachment growing to him. I feel my heart cleaving, with my purest love going to my father, yet broken by a budding affection for Mr. Silver. I fear that the fragment that belongs to my father is beginning to shrink; the colors of my memories of him fading. He has become a feeling, a longing I wish I could fulfill.

Mr. Silver is so alive and vibrant—we walk down the street arm in arm with him, and he can name every type of shape and a hundred different hues; he sees shade and light with an artist's eye, and he can draw so well, I envy his talents! Last week at Aunt Rachel's, I showed him a few of my renderings, which he gently corrected in perspective, but praised greatly as well, though I think my talents are limited in that area. Like Marm, he was forced to leave school at a young age, but he has taken on the task of bettering himself, which I know Marm admires in a person more than any other quality.

I feel guilty for liking this man, yet I feel grateful to him for cheering Marm so.

For tonight, I will tie together these fluttering ribbons of feelings and simply enjoy his company.

January 19, 1907

I always feel *outside*, the observer who writes what is happening, and I don't know whether I will ever get *inside*, whether I will truly understand the workings of the field of science. It seems as impossible as understanding the reason we are born and die.

This sense came upon me when I opened the surprise package from my dear Anushka—a copy of *Gray's Anatomy*, along with her brief note:

> *The pursuit of knowledge is happiness, my friend. We women must allow ourselves that.*

I don't know why I'm having such doubts tonight; perhaps it's the waiting—at the office, we wait for this woman doctor to read our case, we wait for the police to join in, we wait to catch Mary, who is still at large and still spreading disease, we think. These things make me feel once again like everything is going on above me, and I am anxious to climb high enough, to climb *inside*, to see it.

This *Gray's Anatomy* looks very much like the one that used to be in Anushka's father's bookshop—I remember when we discovered it in the back. I finger the pages; the pictures seem so much more complex to me now. I suppose we were immature then and didn't understand what we were looking at. We whispered the strange names of the male and female body parts (with her father working ten feet away!) and our wonder—what must it be like to cut open a body and peer inside at all the intestines and bones and muscles? To see the innards with such detail, to know each and every part, and their functions, no matter how coarse, yes, this is what a scientist must learn.

Looking at the book, I still feel the thrill, but the journey to the true, deep knowledge I would need to be in the sciences seems so much longer and farther to me now.

January 22, 1907

I met the famous woman doctor. Contrary to my imaginings of her, she was neither thick nor ugly. In fact, she doesn't fit so easily into a simple description at all.

She came into our office after having read over the records of Mary Mallon. I was sitting at my desk, and she sat in front of my chief, and they began to discuss the case. Though I set to the task of noting their discussion of our next plan of action, my eyes would not leave her—the stiffness of her forest green skirt suit, her brown curls, her silver spectacles, even the smell of cold air that clung to her fascinated me. She was younger than I thought she'd be, perhaps the age of Anushka's friend Ida, and with that mature manner. At one point, during a mention of me in the conversation, she turned and frankly looked back at me over her wire-rimmed spectacles, but before I could look away, she smiled warmly, then returned her attention to Mr. Soper. I could hardly keep note of all they discussed, though my shorthand has improved greatly. Dr. Baker told Mr. Soper about her experience with the illness and death of underfed, neglected infants, and the firm way she has gone about righting the situation. She said she often res-cued babies from drunken parents and she understood these poorer people, their fear of health inspectors, and anyone who threatened their ways of living. She had used direct force in such cases before, she said, and it always worked.

I couldn't picture Dr. Baker forcing Mary to give a sample. Convincing her with clever words, perhaps, but not forcing.

Once the discussion with Mr. Soper was through, Dr. Baker came to my desk where I was scribbling notes. I looked up, caught by the boldness of her manner.

"So you are the one keeping such neat and precise records," she said.

I nodded into the bright light of her scrutiny.

"You seem to truly understand the importance of your data, and how it reflects the situation," she went on, talking to me as if I were an associate. I glanced over at my chief, who wore a small, satisfied smile. He gave me a brief nod, and I returned my gaze to the doctor.

"Yes," I finally said.

"Are you interested in the sciences, Prudence?" she asked.

"Very much so, ma'am," I said.

"Which branch?" she asked.

My tongue froze; I couldn't define for her what I did not know.

"Research? Surgery? Medicine?" she asked. She seemed genuinely curious about the answer.

"Well, ma'am, before I met you, I didn't know there were schools for girls like me," I said. She looked questioningly at me, so I clarified, "I mean, I didn't know girls could go to a science school."

She put her hand to her hip and said, "There certainly are schools for girls like you, Prudence! I wish more girls knew that! The only way for us to progress is by getting out of the factories and going to school."

Her ardent conviction allowed me to dare a question: "May I ask what school you attended, ma'am?"

"I'm a graduate of the Women's Medical College of Pennsylvania," she said.

A medical college especially for women! In Pennsylvania! I tried to imagine what it might be like. I wanted to ask how one found the opportunity, and how one managed the cost, which I guessed was well beyond the twenty-two dollars I had saved so far. But I could only nod.

"Come and visit me in my office sometime," she said. "We'll talk." The corners of her mouth rose into that warm smile.

"I would like to very much, ma'am," I said.

She nodded once to me, and once to Mr. Soper. I knew then why Mr. Briggs had chosen her to reach out to Mary Mallon. The cook would not be able to resist her.

January 23, 1907

The low point we have reached—the huge distance we've traveled away from what is acceptable behavior—pains me. I thought the presence of a woman, of the sensible Dr. Baker, might convince Mary to see the light, but it did not. In fact, our approach to the cook was violent; it leaves me with a great guilt. I think of Mary tonight, the cuts on her face, her hands scratched and blue with cold. Her wrenching screams. I must ask myself over and over—was it necessary, what we did?

The day started with a shadow of what was to come. Dr. Baker, Mr. Soper, and I met on the pavement in front of the department and the police wagon pulled up. An officer stepped out to open the back for us, a hulking man with a crooked nose and pinched eyes that seemed dead to me. I know some policemen, like Officer Donnell who walks the beat in our neighborhood, but this fellow wasn't like Officer Donnell. In his stiff blue suit and tall hat and copper star, his size and strength seemed to make everything around him shrink. I climbed into the wagon first, trying to avoid his thick-pored face. Did the department really think we needed such a brute to help us get samples from Mary?

The good doctor climbed in beside me, and Mr. Soper squeezed in opposite us.

In the back of the chilly wagon were two empty benches which had held hooligans and outlaws; driving was another officer whose wide neck matched the first. We rode to an ornate West Side brownstone and tied up horses and wagon. The front yard was scattered with children's sleds, toys, and a scraggly snowman (we had a fall, three inches of snow).

Dr. Baker walked up the steps alone while we waited on the sidewalk. I pictured Mary flinging open the door and charging after her with a knife, and felt a bit relieved to have the officers with us. The doctor rang the bell. An elderly maidservant answered, and the doctor introduced herself and asked for Mary Mallon. The woman took one look at the group of us and said she'd be right back. She closed the door on Dr. Baker without inviting her in.

We waited a minute. Then two. Then five. Dr. Baker rang again.

The door opened, and another servant stuck his head out, a small old man, who apologized that no one was in at the present time. He took a step back as if to retreat. Dr. Baker threw out her arm and pushed the door wider, nearly knocking him out of the way. She nodded to us at the bottom of the stairs.

"I'm afraid I'm going to have to ask these officers to search the premises for Mary Mallon," Dr. Baker said. She backed the old fellow into the hall.

The officers started up the stairs.

My heart froze; I now saw clearly what she meant by force.

The old man tried to stop her: "But no one is here, missus—"

"We shall see for ourselves," Dr. Baker said. She disappeared into the house. The officers went in after her.

Mr. Soper followed the officers.

My stomach wrenched; I didn't want to take part in this invasion. I hesitated—then, against my better judgment, I hurried up the stairs after them.

The overcast morning shed little light into the rooms.

I could hear worried servants pretending to help Dr. Baker, but instead merely obstructing the way, pulling up carpets, misdirecting her.

"Well, you know, our employer should be back shortly. She went to take the children to their grandmama's. If you want to wait in the parlor—"

"Sure, Mary came in this mornin', but I think she stepped out—"

"No, I saw her in the drawing room—"

"Yes, she was in the pantry—"

The officers pushed past the servants and climbed the stairs to the second floor of the brownstone, while Mr. Soper followed the doctor back to the kitchen. I felt wrong; I held back. I thought we would get caught at any minute and would be unable to explain ourselves, traipsing through this house without proper invitation.

Yet my feet dragged me forward, into the kitchen, where Dr. Baker seemed untroubled by moral thoughts. She held her hand near the stove and pointed to the water steaming on it, and the cuts of meat laid out on the chopping block.

"I don't think this household is big enough for two cooks, do you?" Dr. Baker asked us, raising her eyebrows over her spectacles.

I could not believe what she did next.

The doctor began to open the wide cabinets under the sink. Mr. Soper looked in the pantry. I was nearly paralyzed by their audacity until Mr. Soper said, "Give a hand, Prudence; we must find her!"

The sharpness in his voice shut off my surprised thoughts. I checked the wood room, the broom closet, and even opened the icebox. I looked in closets and under chairs and in trunks. Overhead we could hear the policemen's feet tromping from room to room, calling warnings for Mary. I looked out the window to the backyard.

Footprints in the snow.

"Look!" I called to Mr. Soper.

He came beside me and tilted his head forward. The yard was fenced-in, with a gate opening out to the back road. Surrounding this yard were the backs of other brownstones, the long rectangles of other yards. The footprints were varied, and many.

"There's a good chance she's out there," he said.

We found the back door, unlocked it, and let ourselves out. Children's footsteps led around the swing set, the garden furniture, and the bird fountain; adult footsteps led to the coal cellar (which was empty of all but coal), the wood pile (behind which no one hid), and out the back gate, where they quickly melted into dozens of other footsteps in the road.

Mary could have hidden in any of the neighboring homes.

Dr. Baker followed us out to the back, her hands on her waist, her breath steaming from her mouth.

"I refuse to believe she's disappeared," she said.

The policemen joined us out back, and we moved to the neighboring yards and knocked on doors, inquiring after our escapee cook. I kept close to my chief, while Dr. Baker ventured out on her own, and the officers separated. We looked everywhere, under tarps, in treehouses, behind woodsheds; in all the yards near our brownstone. I was becoming used to this willful trespass, this disregard for the law a copper star gave us. Our officers *were* the law.

A cry went up from a yard nearly a block down, "Police! Police!" I recognized Dr. Baker's voice. We all went running toward her; she stood beside a brick stairway that had a passage and a small iron door underneath. We stood, expecting to see Mary.

"There!" The doctor pointed to a crack where a piece of blue gingham fluttered.

One of the officers went to the door and flung it open.

Mary stood shivering, her lips pale blue from the cold. The officer reached for her; she leapt out and scratched at his cheek. She ran down the yard. The other officer tackled her; she fell face-first into the snow. The policeman wrestled with her on the ground, trying to grab her hands, pushing her cheek down.

She screamed: "Don't touch me! I'm innocent! Maggots! Lousy cheats! Get yer hands off me! I've done nothing to you!"

I could hardly bear to watch while one copper grabbed her and clapped her wrists together, and the other locked her in cuffs. Her still screaming, "Let me go, let me go!"

Her face and hands were raw and scratched from the scuffle. The first officer hooked her under the shoulders and the second picked her straight up off the ground. They carried her, kicking and screaming, to the wagon. The officer chained her to the bench.

Mary shouted, "Fer God's sake, release me, man! Gutter snakes! Help! Somebody help me, please!"

"Let me sit with her," Dr. Baker said, pushing aside the officers. She lifted her skirts and climbed right in back with Mary, who continued to bellow. People passing by stopped to stare.

"You quiet down now," Dr. Baker said to Mary in a firm tone. "We will take you directly to the hospital, where you will give us a sample of your fluids. Once we have the results, we will release you."

"Let me go! Help! Help me somebody, please!"

Mr. Soper and I boarded the wagon with the screaming woman, and the policemen sped us down to the East River, to the Detention Hospital for Contagious Diseases. By the time we got to the building, Mary had finally settled down like a beaten animal, terror and anger brewing in her red-rimmed eyes.

Dr. Baker admitted Mary for a full bacteriological examination. She was placed in a special room for testing. She wouldn't look at any of us while the officer cuffed her to a chair. She was still breathing heavily and growling to herself, her gingham apron torn, her hair loose from her bun, cheek and knuckles scratched. Anger blew from her like smoke. Looking at her made me want to cry, or turn away, or kneel at her side and explain the whole theory to her, but I stood in the corner, frozen.

Dr. Baker asked a nurse for a basin with warm water and a tray of food. She sat in front of Mary and said to her in a low tone, "We don't want to hurt you, Miss Mallon, you must understand that. You must cooperate with us. Everything will be easier if you cooperate."

She took hold of Mary's hands and bathed them in the warm water, Mary's body stiff in her seat, her face pinched and red.

"If you would relax, we could take off the cuffs and make you more comfortable," Dr. Baker said. She wrapped bandages around Mary's hands and washed the cuts on her face with fresh water.

I could feel Mr. Soper studying Mary. How did he and Dr. Baker find the strength necessary to take the cook from her life the way they had? I questioned my own ability to do what they did. Did I have the stomach for such interference? And was it right? I felt as if we had broken the law. We had no warrant for her arrest, no right to raid her employer's home. Her typhoid was still speculative. Weren't we obliged to release her?

A rail-thin young man, Dr. Parks, joined us.

He looked over his glasses at Mary and asked her, "Miss Mallon, have you ever suffered from the typhoid fever?"

She stared down at her bandaged hands and didn't answer.

"Have you ever had any serious illness, pox, fever, consumption?"

She said nothing. The doctor glanced at us; Mr. Soper shook his head.

"We must take a sample of your blood now," Dr. Parks said.

She tried to jump from the chair, the terror back in her eyes. The two officers pushed her down. Dr. Baker held her arm while Dr. Parks looked for her vein. I pried myself from the corner to help, but could only watch as the needle pierced her skin, her screams filling me with dread.

After, Dr. Parks made her swallow a green fluid laxative.

He spoke about Mary right in front of her, as if she were not there: "Since we are not certain how the disease may be produced in her body, it would be better to test her daily for a time. She's a new sort of case and needs to be observed carefully."

Hearing that, Mary sat straight and said, "I ain't no experiment; you can't do this to me!"

"Miss Mallon, really, it's the only way," Dr. Baker assured her.

"I've got no disease!" she wailed. "Why do you people think I'm sick? Are you crazy? You're all crazy!" She tried to yank free her bandaged hands, shouting, "I'm well! I'm well! Why doesn't anybody believe me?"

She was hurting herself, and our presence wasn't helping.

When the nurse brought Mary her tray of food, the officers stayed with her, and the rest of us stepped from the room. Out in the hallway, we could still hear her crying.

Dr. Parks said to us, "A person who learns for the first time that they carry a contagious disease is often upset. Some won't cooperate for days."

"At least she's in quarantine now," Mr. Soper said. "At the very least, she will not be passing the typhoid to that family."

"Give her some time to settle down," Dr. Parks said. "We can discuss her case when we have some evidence, yes?"

I understood then that we would be leaving her there.

Dr. Parks excused himself to do his work, and Dr. Baker left, saying she had other business in the neighborhood. I went out with Mr. Soper into the cold afternoon, and I could feel an emptiness between us as we headed toward the street-car stop, now that we had caught Mary. Besides the obvious question—does she *really* carry the typhoid germ?—there are still so many unknowns to her case. What is her history? Who *is* she, and where has she been? There looms before us the possibility that she may never give us the answers. I suppose my chief was feeling the same emptiness, for at the trolley stop, he gave me the rest of the day off.

"We shall visit her again soon," Mr. Soper said. "We have some deep inquiry still ahead of us."

His face looked so worn and tired, I wanted to touch his cheek and take from him his exhaustion. Instead I watched him walk away, his head bowed.

I can't stop thinking about her piercing screams, the wild terror in her eyes when the police tackled her, the bloody cuts on her face and hands. It's one thing to follow the course of a disease through observation and questioning. It is truly another to be out jailing human beings suspected of carrying germs. To tell the truth, the more I think about what we've done, the sicker I feel. The whole incident was immoral. Is this how the Department of Health and Sanitation goes about preventing disease? Do I really want to be part of such an organization? What if Mary doesn't carry the typhoid? We have already assaulted her and imprisoned her and taken her dignity from her, treating her like a common fugitive from the law.

What will we do if we are wrong?

February 1, 1907

I am human. Despite my desire to be purely scientific, I have sympathies, revulsions, fears. But I want to be *more than* human, *better than* human—I want to be above and see all, to understand the reason for everything. I want to be pure science, pure brain, without so much feeling. Feeling clouds me. And yet I come back to the sad truth: I am human, I cannot help but feel for a woman we've imprisoned, a woman who carries disease and makes people ill.

Tests have revealed it: Mary Mallon carries the typhoid fever bacteria inside her.

It splits me like lightning, this definite news. There can be no doubt about her now. But the way we approached her haunts me, it bothers me to the very center of myself.

Is it right for the department to treat a human being like a contagious disease?

I'm not the only one whose feelings about this are knotted.

Despite Mr. Soper's personal explanation of how he saved the Bowings from this epidemic, they are outraged at our department for entering and searching their home with no legal warrant, for handling their personal belongings, for frightening the servants and dirtying their floors, and for removing Mary so abruptly and imprisoning her with no apparent reason (Mary is not sick, they insist, and could not possibly be responsible for the department's claims). They demand an apology from the mayor himself and from every single politician who controls a city office, Republican and Tammany. They want the immediate release of Mary Mallon as they say she is being held illegally. Even Mr. Briggs has tried to respond to their fury with fact, but the family has righteousness on their side and won't have the department bullying them.

Dr. Parks gives us results over the telephone daily:

Positive.

Positive.

Positive.

Eight days, including the weekend, and all of Mary's tests, the blood and feces, every single one comes out positive for typhoid. And every day after he receives the call, Mr. Soper replaces the handset on its hooks and stares at it. He folds his fingers and looks at them. I can almost feel his helplessness. I sense he is evaluating difficult questions: What do we do with her now? How do we treat her? Where should we keep her?

How do we explain this to people outside the department?

We went to the hospital for a further interview with her. I was ashamed to visit her, yet I also felt compelled, as if I might be able to see something in her I didn't see before. Dr. Parks led us to the ward where he had put her with the consumptive population, where he says she is least likely to be affected by the others who are quarantined, and they her. The sound of all those women with that special tubercular cough, wet lungs ripping, and the spit of blood after, echoed through the hall.

Mary lay on her metal bed, a woman to either side of

her, the pall of misery shadowing her face so gray, I could scarcely look at her. The bandages had been removed from her hands, and she picked at her scabs constantly. I wanted to reach out and still her nervous fingers. To say something kind to her. She had lost weight and did not raise her head to look at us.

Mr. Soper tapped the hat in his hand and sighed, glancing at me with troubled eyes. I shook my head at him; neither of us had wanted things to go this way.

He sat on the chair beside Mary's bed and spoke to her in a quiet voice. "Miss Mallon, we have come here to speak to you today because we want to explain your significance in the passage of this pervasive bacteria. You are the first person we have encountered whom we have definitely confirmed to be a healthy carrier of the typhoid germ. It's important we trace the genesis of your disease."

She stopped picking at her hands and smoothed her skirt against her leg. "I've got no disease," she said.

Mr. Soper squeezed his eyes shut for a moment. He opened them and said, "I'm afraid the facts are clear in this case. We have determined with daily testing that you are indeed carrying the typhoid germ. Do you remember ever contracting the fever, Miss Mallon?"

"Never been sick in me life."

"As a child, maybe?"

Mary stretched on the bed and hugged her pillow to her face.

"Even a mild case, perhaps back in your native land?"

She did not answer.

"Miss Mallon, the more we know, the better we can help you and perhaps remove the disease from you," Mr. Soper said.

It was clear that she refused to believe the typhoid was living inside her. After a few more questions, Mr. Soper sighed; I packed up my notes and we went to see Dr. Parks.

In his office, Dr. Parks told us he was giving her Professor Herman's Systematic Relief. A tincture of belladonna and chloride, thirteen drops in hot water six times a day, was supposed to kill the germ. He didn't know when it would start working.

"It's like many of these contagious diseases," Dr. Parks said. He teetered his hand edge to edge in the air. "All we can do is wait."

Mr. Soper nodded, his eyes cast down.

"However, we have discovered one thing about Mary," the doctor added.

My chief looked up; I licked my pencil to write.

"The nurses learned that she came here from Ireland when she was fourteen after both her parents died. She crossed the Atlantic alone."

"How did her parents die?" Mr. Soper asked.

The doctor shook his head. "That's it, that's all she would say."

Mr. Soper rubbed his fingers together, thinking. "It would help us so much if she would talk about her past," he said.

"We can't force her to talk," Dr. Parks said.

Mr. Soper sighed. "No, I don't suppose we can."

We bid the doctor good day. As I followed Mr. Soper out of the hospital, I imagined Mary Mallon at fourteen losing both of her parents, and the terrible sadness she must have felt. Still, somehow, she managed to travel by herself to America, probably on one of those giant steamers the companies pack with as many people as will fit. A girl alone, with all those strangers pressed against her—the thought makes me cold. She must surely have gotten seasick in the middle of the ocean. Who comforted her? Did she make any friends? When she landed here, how did she find a job and a place to sleep? Maybe she started as a scullery maid in a kitchen and observed the cook, learning as she went. I pictured her, a red-haired girl hardened by her difficult circumstances, fighting for every scrap of food, nothing coming easily.

I understood Mary suddenly, knowing that small bit of her past. I understood her bitterness and her tenaciousness and her anger.

Over supper, I spoke with Marm about the whole case. She blew on her soup, thinking. So much has changed in our lives since I started this job, and I think she wanted to be careful about advising me. After a while, she said, "It's going to be hard for you to believe that what you're doing is right, Prudence, because you're a pioneer, and you don't know what lies ahead."

"It seems like no one knows," I said. "No one understands why a healthy woman carries the typhoid inside her. No one knows how to help her."

"That's why they're keeping her in quarantine, so they can study her," Marm said.

I've thought long and hard about Marm's answer. I'm not sure I have the strength to study Mary like a pinned insect long enough to solve her case. Even remembering the girls who died from Mary's cooking doesn't help when I see her on a ward full of consumptives. Dying women who cough out contagion with every breath, yet Mary is bursting with health! Couldn't she catch their disease? What can we do to protect her? She can't go back into the world. She can't stay where she is. It is this place of purgatory that disturbs me.

I long to push myself above human feeling and into science. Yet I can't see with a cold eye. I don't know if I am fit for this life of the mind as I had once thought I was.

February 6, 1907

Last night I had a terrible nightmare. Mary had escaped from quarantine and was fleeing through the city streets, smearing disease over crowds, people falling ill in her wake as if in a plague. Somehow I spotted her and followed her to Mr. Soper's home, a place of brilliant light. He slept peacefully in a gauzy bed. Mary stood over him with that wild, trapped look in her eyes. Suddenly he awoke, and seeing Mary, sat straight up in a fright.

She wailed, "Why are you tormenting me?" in a most wrenching voice, then she opened her mouth horribly wide, and I could see the round typhoid germs bubbling up from inside her.

She saw me and screamed: "You!"

I ran down a bright hall, the sound of Mary's feet pounding after me. I feared for Mr. Soper, whom I had left behind. I knew he had succumbed to the fever. I was crying and calling his name, turning corners, barely dodging Mary each time. The bends and steps of the house were endless. I ran until I couldn't breathe and then collapsed on the floor, sobbing with the little breath I had.

Mary came behind me, pleading, "Help me, girl! Don't lock me up! Don't put me away! I beg of you, please! Help me!"

I tried to get up, but she kept pushing me down and begging, begging without end.

I woke to find myself on the floor, my back pressed into the cold stove.

Dread sank into my bones; I felt sick. The image of her filled with typhoid germs has not left me all day. Feelings of death and helplessness, fears too deep for me to name, swell inside me. The sense of loss bleeds through me.

And what happened with Mr. Soper today makes my ache more real.

This afternoon Mr. Soper received a mysterious telephone call. I was working at my desk, transcribing his study of Mary's case, only half listening to his replies. Expecting the report from Dr. Parks, I noticed a stiffening of my chief's body and a lowering of his voice. I glanced furtively at him, wondering if it was the Bowing family, still so upset with our trespass. Usually Mr. Soper deals with them in a calm, short manner, but this time, color flushed his cheeks. He asked the speaker to wait a moment, and held his hand over the horn.

"Prudence," he said, "will you please fetch me a sheaf of paper from the supply closet?"

"I have some here," I said. I reached into my desk.

"And ink. Please go to the supply closet right now and get me a bottle of black India ink," he said, indicating the door. "Please go."

I rose from my desk, watching him. He wanted to take the call alone. He had never done that before. Was it a woman?

The forbidden love I kept bottled so tightly rushed into my throat, and I left the room.

Choking on jealousy, I closed the door quietly and stood just outside the glass, trying to hear what my chief was saying without seeming obvious to the fellows who passed me in the hall. I needed to find out who was on the telephone. I heard "a private matter," and "not authorized to speak," and "Mr. Briggs," things that were enough to tell me it was a business call.

But the poison had been released in me.

Love flooded my chest and ached in my stomach. I hurried down the hall to the supply closet, gulping back the fear that I had lost him. My hands shook as I unlocked the door. I stood looking at the shelves of paper and pens, inks and blotters, white stars of light dancing before my eyes. I worked so hard to hide my love from him, to remember Anushka's three rules, but underneath everything I did, during every moment of the day, it was there. The power of it, now released, nearly overcame me. I drank down air, trying to fit my feeling back into the small, secret box where it belonged.

But it wouldn't go.

It's like walking to the center of a bridge and looking out over a long, wide river and trying to fit that vastness into a small box. I had managed it somehow before.

Now it just won't go.

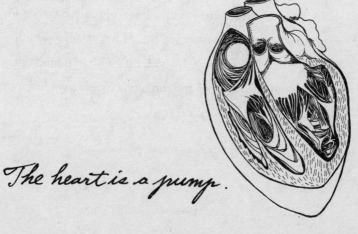

The heart is a pump.

February 8, 1907

I sit in the office every day with my chief, all my nerve cells exposed, sensitive to his every move and word. I wish I could talk to someone about these emotions, to free myself from them somehow. My letters to Anushka no longer seem like enough. I need to talk to another girl, to hear her advice, but there is no one. My mind wanders to Marm, but I cannot speak to her about this poisoned side of me. I think of Dr. Baker; inside me, I find a lingering anger at her for treating Mary Mallon so poorly. Still, I wonder how she has managed her own feelings. I wonder if being in a man's profession has made her cold and forceful. Could I ever learn to be like that?

February 10, 1907

I visited Dr. Baker today. On my lunch break, I excused myself from the office and slipped upstairs, to the fourth floor, to talk to her. I felt I needed some answers. Not about Mr. Soper, but about myself. Answers only she could give me.

The fourth floor is a long hall, rooms with glass doors on either side. Girls fill delivery baskets with cream and eggs at one table; at another, white-dressed nurses tend to infants with dirty faces, rag-clad mothers hovering nearby. On the wall, a sign reads, HELP A CHILD, GIVE TO THE NEEDY.

At the far end of the hall, Dr. Baker sat in an office, her name stenciled across the clear glass door. Seeing her, I felt what I might become one day, a woman with her own office in a world of medicine. Then I caught the distress in her eyes. Across the desk from her a dandy twirled his hat with one hand and brandished a cigar with the other. I couldn't hear their words through the closed door, but I worried for her and revealed my presence through the window. Her face brightened when she saw me, and she nodded and waved as if she'd been waiting for me. She excused herself to the man, got up, and opened the door for me.

"Come in, please come in, Prudence," she said, ushering me in. She said to the man, "Yes, so, that's really all I can tell you now."

He stood slowly, looking suspiciously from her to me. "I'll hear back from you soon?" he asked.

"Oh, quite soon," she said.

Words seemed to gather in his mouth, but none came out. He turned and left the office.

Dr. Baker sighed and returned to her desk. "Please, sit," she said to me.

The chair was still warm from the man. I slid to the edge and folded my hands, nearly overcome by the cheap cologne and cigar stink in the air.

Dr. Baker touched her curls, took off her spectacles, and wiped them clean. Her bare face surprised me, the thin skin around her eyes, the weakness of her vision. I did not think she contained such frailty. I wanted to ask about the man, but it was not my place. Returning her glasses to her nose, it was as if her strength had returned. She looked at me expectantly and asked how she could help me.

"I want to talk to you about—about school," I said.

"Ah," she said, and smiled. "It would do my heart good to have you join the women's cause."

I didn't know what she meant by the cause. Perhaps she was talking about the suffragettes. I've seen them march in the streets in order to gain the vote and women's rights. Their voices are loud, and with their arms hooked together in protest, they don't seem afraid of anything. Marm also calls them pioneers, setting the way for other women to follow.

"How old are you, Prudence?" Dr. Baker asked.

"I'm almost seventeen."

"And where do you attend school now?"

"Ma'am, I left to take this job," I said.

She picked up the ink pen on her desk and tapped the end of it against her blotter. It was as if something in her moved away from me.

"Does Mr. Soper know you left?" she asked.

"I mentioned it at my first interview, ma'am. But I told him I could work, so he hired me."

"Well, that seems neglectful of him," she said. "I thought he was more interested in your future—"

"It's not his fault, ma'am. It was my own decision to leave school. I did go to Mrs. Browning herself and try to plead with her to let me continue my schooling at the same time. But she wouldn't, so I left."

"Mrs. Browning?" the doctor repeated. "Did you attend Mrs. Browning's School for Girls?"

I nodded.

"Why would a girl with your scientific skills go to a vocational school, of all places?"

"My mother didn't want me to go to Free School," I said. "She thought Mrs. Browning's would give me a better chance in life than she had. She doesn't want me to end up a midwife like her."

Dr. Baker's eyebrows raised. "Your mother's a midwife?"

"Yes," I said. "I spent last summer helping her."

"So, you've done some doctoring." Dr. Baker smiled. "And now you want to go to medical school?"

I had never thought of my work with Marm as doctoring.

"I'm not sure," I said.

"Is that so?" Dr. Baker's eyes urged the truth from me.

"Ma'am, it's just . . . this case with Mary Mallon has got me questioning myself," I said.

"Questioning, how?" she asked.

I spoke delicately, but something in me trusted I could be honest. "Well, ma'am, when I started working for Mr. Soper, I saw illness as a kind of weed, something that could be found and cleaned away. I didn't think it could live inside a person without sickening or killing them, not like with Mary. Now it's as if the disease and the person are inseparable. When the police officer threw Mary in the snow and they locked her up, they were treating *her* like a disease. But she's a person, she has feelings. I can't seem to think about the case without thinking about her, too."

The doctor looked at me as if she was evaluating my words, then she laughed one short bark; I was relieved at her laughter, though I didn't understand it.

"That's exactly what they try to teach you in medical school," she said. "Compassion."

"But I can't pull apart what she feels and what I feel, ma'am."

"That will come with time," Dr. Baker said. "You'll learn to see the larger picture."

I wished I felt as confident as she did.

"Do you understand the need for quarantine, Prudence?" Dr. Baker looked hard at me. I didn't have an answer. She said, "Keeping Mary at a safe distance from the public is the difference between one person's temporary discomfort and hundreds falling ill. Disease is a removable evil—that is the motto of our department. Mary carries the typhoid, Prudence. There is no way around that fact."

I wanted to ask her if she thought Mary herself was evil because she carried disease, but something in her face kept me quiet.

Her eyes relaxed.

"You are an observant girl, your notes are thoughtful and clear, you seem to care about people. You have a wonderfully curious mind. You know, Prudence, I think you'd make a fine doctor," she said.

Her words warmed me, like hands holding me. It was the strong opinion I longed for, the outside view I'd been seeking. She presented me with my innocent self again, the girl who wanted to do something meaningful with her life.

Then my memories returned, of what we had done to Mary, of my own weak emotions. My doubts came back quick and strong.

"Medical school is the most difficult kind of education,"

Dr. Baker went on. "It involves the study of many subjects, and you will have to cut open bodies and handle inner organs. In order to succeed, you must want it more than anything."

When I took this job, I wanted to see a cell in the microscope more than anything. But now that I've seen so many other disturbing things, I'm just not so sure what I want anymore.

Dr. Baker sat back in her chair, folding her hands against her waist.

"It wasn't easy seeing Mary in that police wagon," I said quietly.

"Our actions were for the greater good, Prudence. Surely you must see that, for all your reservations. We have stopped the spread of disease. As a doctor, you must make impossible decisions and face terrible odds. You have to know whether you can do that or not."

I nodded, wondering if I would ever see things the way she did.

"It's a slow process, learning about the human body and what makes us sick," she said gently. "It's even slower discovering ways to cure us. If we knew how to rid Mary of the typhoid germ, we would be able to release her. We need good brains to help figure these things out, brains like yours."

I had come to her with the intention of finding answers; instead I felt even more confused. She said I had the ability to become a doctor. But I didn't know if I had the heart.

The air felt uncomfortable suddenly. I cleared my throat and said I thought Mr. Soper might be looking for me. I thanked her and stood and went to the door and bid her good day.

February 13, 1907

My life is changing before my very eyes. Less than a year ago, I was sitting next to my best friend at school, trading notes with her about the silly lessons we were learning, and afterwards, shopping at the pushcarts together for supper groceries and talking about plans for our lives. She wanted to marry a writer of books—living above her father's bookstore gave her that. Imagine being married to one, she'd say, the stories he could tell you! Now she's in love with an older man, a farmer, no less. She would've laughed last year if I had divined her future the way it has turned out.

And what did I want? To see my father again, to understand how the world works, why the sky is blue and why dogs walk on four legs. I never would've guessed I'd have a job where I could use my brain to its very utmost capacity. I didn't think I would ever love a man, and that he would turn out to be my chief. I didn't dream I could have the chance to be a doctor. Yet—I'm ashamed to say it—I am afraid. I fear going away to a school in Pennsylvania, far from Marm and Mr. Soper. What would happen to me there? Would I be able to understand the lessons? Would I fail and lose everything?

I don't know if I have the courage for this challenge Dr. Baker has presented me.

My family is made of pioneers. My grandfather left his home with his baby and his wife and came to America. What did it take for him to do that? He left his own parents, and his aunts, uncles, cousins, nieces and nephews, a language he knew, a farm he loved. My father left a wife and young child to go to another country and fight a war. I don't see how my family members tore themselves from the lives and people they loved, in order to press themselves into a new mold.

Why does a person have to leave so much behind when they make one decision over another?

February 15, 1907

I found myself seeking out an old classmate this evening, a girl who has known me for much of my life. My meeting with her was revealing; in a way, she showed me where I belong.

Mr. Soper sent me out of the office early so he could have a private talk with yet another strange man, which I must confess I did not like. It disturbs me when he keeps things from me.

I wandered up Sixth Avenue in the orange sunset, not wanting to go straight home. I followed the springtime hints of snowmelt and soil, longing for someone to talk to. I felt as if I were one of a swarm of creatures, all drawn upwards in the same direction. I passed the shoemaker's and the butcher's and the baker's, and all the office buildings that line the avenue. I looked into the faces of the winter-weary with curiosity. I'd been so absorbed in my own life, I had forgotten that others existed. I felt desirous of something fresh—a scent, an item of clothing. Weaving in and out of stores on the avenue, I purchased a scone, but it didn't fill me. My hunger was not for food. Upon reaching 34th Street, I glanced in the windows of Macy's and thought I saw Josephine at the counter. I stared, unsure; I entered the department store and found it was another girl, similarly tall and pretty. I inquired after Josephine, and the girl told me Jo was in a family way and had been let go.

I suddenly wanted to see her.

I went to her East Side apartment, where her mother told me she had moved to the West Side with her husband, Willem Stryker. As I seemed to be on a mission, I jumped onto the nearest omnibus and rode west.

I knocked at the door of her townhouse, and Josephine herself answered; we looked at each other without speaking. Her extreme plumpness and the green tinge about her face shocked me.

"Prudence," she said finally. "What are you doing here?"

I shrugged and shook my head, strangely happy to see her.

"Well, come in. I was just about to settle down for some tea," she said.

She showed me to a pretty, lacy paradise of a parlor. On

her finger, diamonds sparkled, and for a moment I wanted what she had—a rich husband, a quiet place to read, long, empty days of waiting.

A serving girl came in with tea and white cookies; Josephine popped a whole sweet into her mouth and chewed and giggled. "These cookies are the only thing that make me feel better," she said. "Cookies and ice cream and sweet potatoes. Everything else makes me sick."

"You must drink milk and eat plenty of raw meat to have a good baby," I told her.

"Ugh, meat, I can't even stand to smell it," she said.

"And when the baby comes, you must have your nurse feed it a mix of raw eggs and cow's milk," I said. "Keep it fat and healthy."

She stuck another cookie in her mouth and tilted her head, crunching and looking at me. "You work for your mother the midwife, don't you?" she asked.

"I used to," I said. I was surprised she remembered.

"Do you think she could tend to me?" she asked.

"Doesn't your family have someone?"

"The lady my mama used died. Will's mother wants me to go to Sloane's, but I'd rather use your mother, if she can take me. Maybe you can come too," she said.

She couldn't hide her fear of childbirth; she seemed very alone. I wanted to promise her I'd help her, but I thought of my job, and how Mr. Soper needed me.

"If you can, Prudence, I would feel so much safer with you there," she added.

I nodded, and I wondered what her life was truly like, being married and with child at the age of seventeen. Was it as easy as I assumed? Did her husband treat her kindly?

"How is Willem Stryker?" I asked.

She chewed another cookie, looking me over.

"You've never been in love, have you, Prudence?" she said.

I saw how she viewed me—a dull girl with her nose stuck in a book, a brain without a heart. How I wanted to tell her about Mr. Soper, and the feelings that so troubled me! How I wanted to free the ache that lived with me day and night!

"Love makes everything else seem unimportant." She sighed.

I looked at the surface of her shiny, pretty eyes. Her words started a fresh pain in me; I wanted to push her away, to leave her. I could not tell her about my feelings.

"I must think about my studies," I blurted.

"What studies?" she asked.

"At the Department of Health and Sanitation, where I work, there is a woman doctor. She has encouraged me—"

"A woman doctor!" Jo exclaimed. She laughed. "Yes, of course. You've always been a doctor, Prudence, the way you study those books, like there's actually something interesting in there!"

I smiled and lowered my eyes, taken aback by her outburst.

She said, "I remember in school you spent whole days just staring out the window, a cloud of thoughts above your head that no one else could see. Yet when our teacher asked you a question about the lesson, why, you could turn to her and always give the right answer. None of us ever knew how you did that."

I looked at Josephine; in school I had been so unhappy. I was different. I had spent most days imagining I was somewhere else.

In a flash, I recalled my conversation with Dr. Baker. She talked about the cause, about girls who marched in the streets. They did not sit around thinking; they changed the world. But maybe they had started out like me, as doubtful, questioning girls, girls who longed to use their minds for a good and meaningful purpose. No matter how difficult a choice that might be.

"There is a women's medical college, in Pennsylvania," I said.

"You'll be Dr. Galewski," Jo said.

It seemed so clear to her.

"Dr. Galewski," I repeated softly.

Yes, that is who I will be.

Josephine clapped her hands and laughed. "A woman doctor," she said, "how *that* will turn Mrs. Browning's stomach!"

A warm grin started in my chest; it floated up through me and lifted the corners of my mouth. I rose to my feet, feeling lighter than I had in days.

"I will return soon with my mother to check on your progress," I said.

I would start my doctoring, as Dr. Baker calls it, with Josephine.

Dr. Prudence Galewski

Doctor Galewski

Dr. P. Galewski

Doctor P. Galewski

The New York American

FEBRUARY 16, 1907   FIVE CENTS

GERMS OF TYPHOID CARRIED FOR LIFE—PRESENCE KEPT A SECRET

A case shrouded in mystery by the Department of Health and Sanitation has revealed that a woman cook suspected of carrying the typhoid fever inside her healthy body has been locked up for the better part of a month with no chance for freedom.

Mary Mallon, hired as cook by a dozen wealthy families in the New York City area, was captured at her place of employ late January. Mr. Herman Briggs, superintendent of the department, authorized Mr. George Soper and Dr. Sara Baker to raid the Bowing residence without a warrant in search of this human typhoid germ.

Miss Prudence Galewski was on hand to help Officers Kevan and Hill arrest and imprison the poor, helpless cook, treating her like a criminal for possibly carrying disease, despite her obviously healthy state. The cook is presently being held at the Detention Hospital on the East River.

One unnamed source at the hospital says the department claims that up to forty people may have fallen ill from food Miss Mallon prepared, but nothing has been proven as of yet. According to several of the families she cooked for, her meals were tasty and satisfying.

———————

February 16, 1907

Reading this article, I feel stunned, sickened, queasy. I feel as if we were under physical attack from an enemy who wanted nothing more than to breed hatred and contempt for our department. We seem like fools mistreating an innocent woman. Where is the truth in that? Where are the real details of this story?

But I am not the one to talk to those reporters, who swim like sharks in front of our doors.

Early this morning, after the story broke, several men from other newspapers gathered about on the pavement in front of our building, hungry for a story. As I walked up the steps, a man came to me and pushed his pencil and pad into my face.

"Miss Prudence Galewski, is it true that you had a hand in the capture and arrest of Mary Mallon, the human typhoid germ carrier?" he shouted at me.

I tried to pass him, stunned by his question, by his use of my name. He planted himself in front of me and would not budge.

"Miss Galewski, does the department really have proof that this woman carries disease?"

The way he shouted made me want to shield my head, to run from him.

"Is it true you're treating an innocent woman like a criminal? A criminal, Miss Galewski?"

I could not breathe; tears gathered in my eyes, a burn began in my stomach. He would not step aside to let me through. The other reporters crowded me, throwing words at me. Like a pack of wolves biting into me. I covered my ears and bowed my head, hoping they would go away.

Suddenly, from behind, I felt hands on my arms, grabbing me, pushing me around the man. I heard: "Leave her alone!" I tried to see who it was, but the hands guided me through the crowd. "Outta the way, give us room!" he demanded. This man directed me up the stairs and to my office, where he released me. I saw the face of the science fellow who had tormented me. Jonathan. I wanted to holler at him for touching me and thank him for saving me at the same time. I could not stop shaking. He walked away before I could collect my senses.

All the months we worked to find Mary, all that we went through, boiled down to this one article. Now I know who the strange men were in our office, talking to Mr. Soper and Dr. Baker. I don't understand why my chief and the doctor didn't show them our notes or the test results, or explain the steps we went through, or the theory itself.

Or maybe they did.

Our superintendent is outraged; he can't believe the brazenness of the press, and the way they twisted the facts. He called a meeting this evening; everyone involved in the case attended, even Dr. Parks and the policemen who brought Mary in.

"We will give them no more information, since they don't know how to treat it properly," Mr. Briggs said. He's a small, nervous man, but his voice boomed, "I don't want *any* of you talking to *anyone* about this case. Not a name, not a place, not a single fact! That's it! Not a word!"

We found out that it was the Bowings, the family Mary worked for, who went to the newspaper looking for public sympathy.

Before I left work tonight, I saw that Mr. Briggs had ordered men to be stationed in front of our building. We now have police guarding our doors.

February 22, 1907

The newspaper articles about Mary Mallon and our work have mushroomed, with a new crop of falsehoods every day. The *Herald* article named me as a medical intern, and the *Sun* said Mary Mallon has been removed from the city entirely, to a hidden destination in New Jersey. I am now famous in the neighborhood thanks to the papers, and I wake up with a stomachache every morning. Her Majesty Zanberger calls me into her stuffy, cabbagey apartment and tries to get gossip out of me. She has begun a scrapbook, which she shows to anyone who'll stop long enough to look. "Everyone's so proud of you," she says, "and we want to know all about this human typhoid germ."

Of course, I cannot and do not tell her anything.

Where I was once the observer, now I am the observed. This attention is like a constant bright ray in my eyes that I cannot shut off. It's painful and upsetting, all the personal questions, the probes into my privacy. Miss Lara pinned me to the vegetable cart to ask when I had attended medical school. Our butcher, Mr. Barren, withheld meat from me. He wanted to know where exactly this Germ Lady was imprisoned, and wouldn't give me the soup bones unless I told. He seemed very nervous about me touching the meat cases, as if I myself carried disease.

Once false stories are printed in the newspapers, my neighbors believe them. It's impossible to correct every misstatement, especially since I'm forbidden to speak about the case.

Seeing my name in the newspapers has changed me down deep. It's given me a sense of responsibility, it's made me see how important the truth is.

I wish there was a way to tell the truth. To make people understand.

Mary Mallon has been moved to a hospital on North Brother Island, between Queens and the Bronx, just a short ferry ride away. Mr. Briggs had her moved right after the first article appeared. This place affords the doctors the privacy to study her properly. They are contemplating removing Mary's gallbladder, which they suspect is the culprit in producing the typhoid germs. I worry about this sort of experimentation with her; I think of the nightmare I had, her pleading with me to protect her. Mr. Soper assures me they will first try every other manner to cure her, as stomach surgery is fraught with the possibility of infection, for which there is no cure. There is no proof it would work, he says, but it may be her only choice, if she wants to return to her previous life.

Perhaps that's what makes this case so hard to explain to other people.

How do I tell them: We are not sure how to treat her?

We don't know how to cure her.

All we know is that she mustn't cook for anyone.

March 1, 1907

Finally I found the right moment to tell Marm my decision about medical school. Our attention had been drawn to the newspapers, and maybe I was a little frightened of what she might say.

Last night she looked so sweet, warming her knees by the stove, sewing a new bag for her midwifery instruments. I leaned on the arm of her chair and took one of her curls in my finger. My throat tensed; the words tangled there. I worried she'd be unhappy with me for wanting to go so far from her. I feared the cost would be too much for us. I didn't want to burden her in any way.

But I made myself speak. "Marm, I wanted to tell you about Dr. Baker. The woman doctor in the department?"

"Hmmm?" Marm continued her sewing.

I went on, "Well, she has presented me with the possibility of attending medical school."

Marm blinked up at me, shaking her head. I let go of her curl. She put her work aside. I stepped back a little.

"I haven't discussed it further with Dr. Baker, because I wanted to talk it over with you. But I think I want to go."

"Medical school?" she asked. "How is that possible?"

I couldn't tell if she was upset or . . . or something else.

"There's a college in Pennsylvania that takes girls," I told her. "That's where Dr. Baker herself went, and she says I could go there too."

Marm had a strange look in her eyes. Suddenly I wavered. Was I doing the right thing?

"I—I wasn't sure I wanted to go. But now—now I am," I said.

She stared at me. My hands began to shake; I clasped my fingers together. Then, I saw them—tears. Marm was crying.

"Marm—oh, Marmy—"

She reached up and pulled me into her arms like a little girl. I knelt to her and held her close to me. I could feel her tears on my shoulder through my sleeve, warm tears that made my eyes hot. We hugged each other tightly.

"You make me so proud," she said.

Those words plunged into my heart, filling me with joy.

I held my breath and listened to her weep, feeling my

own tears slide down my face. I felt her whole body shake, and the strength of her arms as she clung to me. Proud of me—she was proud of me. The wonder of that struck me, all that she's done for me, all that she's given up for me, all that she has allowed me to do, to be. Then I saw why she cried—she had sacrificed for her children, she had lost one of us, I was all she had left. And I had done something to make her proud. I felt a great warmth in my chest, an honor. She honored me with her pride.

She released me, finally, and wiped her cheeks, and patted mine. I stood and slipped into my chair and took up the newspaper to hide my still trembling lip. I heard Marm pick up her sewing.

She is proud of me. Does she know how much that means to me? Does she know how closely she has guided my life, and how grateful I am to her for such a show of care? Looking at her, I see how I might be if I had a daughter of my own with the man I love—I would want for her everything I could not have for myself. I see now why people have children—to extend themselves, to become more than what they could be alone.

I vow to do my very best to be a worthy part of Marm's greater self.

March 2, 1907

Encouraged by Marm's approval, I went upstairs to Dr. Baker's office today to talk to her. She welcomed me in. I took a deep breath and said, "I spoke to my mother about it. I have decided to become a doctor."

Her sober face broke into a gleaming smile. She said, "Oh, Prudence, I'm so pleased. Our profession needs more women like you, with good minds and a firm discipline. I'm positive you'll do well."

I felt all the weight of her expectation and feared she thought Marm would be able to afford it. I had to tell her how impossible that would be. I met her eyes and said, "Dr. Baker, as a midwife, my mother earns very little—"

The doctor held up her hand, stopping me. She said, "If you do well on the entrance examination, there will be occasions for funds donated or lent from prominent families. The

New York moneyed families love to support smart girls like you."

"I *did* have yearly funds to attend Mrs. Browning's," I said. "The first was given to me personally by Mrs. Morgan on my sixth birthday—"

I stopped; I meant to assure her, or myself, but it had the tinny sound of bragging.

"Yes, we could ask the Morgans, or the Vanderbilts, or the Livingstons," she said, leaning back in her chair.

She tapped her fingers together, looking at me with her shrewd eyes, then she turned and reached behind her, pulling a book from her shelf. She held it and said, "But you must do well on the test! In order to pass the entrance examination, you must have an overall understanding of the human system. Begin your studies with this."

She handed me the book. I looked at the title. *The Biology of Man.*

She turned and reached again, this time producing *True Blood Chemistry and the Myth of the Four Humors.*

"In exchange for your diligence, I will tutor you," she said. "We'll start with biology, the blood, and anatomy."

She reached for *Gray's Anatomy.*

When I told her I had a copy of the book at home, she

raised an eyebrow at me with a small smile and took instead *The Effect of Germs in Everyday Life*, a book on the work of Dr. Louis Pasteur.

"There is no time to waste," she said. "People's lives will depend on how well you know your material, Prudence."

I pulled the heavy books from the desk and hugged them to me. I felt as if she had turned a lens inside me and a hundred questions came into focus. How difficult was the test? Where would I take it? Did I have a chance of passing it? Could a girl like me really go to medical school?

As if she knew my questions, Dr. Baker said, "I will help you arrange for travel to Pennsylvania for the test. I have every confidence you will do well on the examination, Prudence, and that they will accept you into the school. I would not have recommended this path to you if I didn't believe that."

Dr. Baker picked up her pen and pulled a stack of papers toward her. I stood, feeling as if she had released me. "When should I come for a tutoring session?" I inquired.

"When you have finished reading those books," she said. "We will discuss the body, then I'll take you into the dispensary and you can visit patients with me."

I thought of those dirty children I saw in the halls, and their sad mothers, and the idea of tending to them—of being given permission to examine them closely—posed a whole new series of questions. What would I see? How would I be of help to them? How did Dr. Baker decide what illness a person suffered from, just by looking at them?

I returned downstairs, distracted by these questions. Mr. Soper showed an instant curiosity about the books I was carrying and asked about them. His nearness and interest sent a blush flaming up my neck.

I looked down at the books, my heart pounding in my throat. "I—I just came from Dr. Baker's office," I said. "She's encouraged me to go medical school."

His eyes took on a warm light; he nodded.

"Is Dr. Baker helping you with the entrance exam?" he asked gently.

"Yes, she is—she will be," I said. My cheeks felt fevered under his gaze.

"Well, if you need further aid, let me know," he said. "I'm an engineer, but I do know a little something about medicine."

How he smiled and looked at me! The kindness in his face—I could barely thank him. Somehow I was able to escape the office this evening without revealing too much emotion. I can hardly allow myself to imagine Mr. Soper helping me to study. What if I make a mistake, or don't remember something? I don't want him to see me falter. And his near-ness would cause a distraction too great for me to overcome.

Despite my ambition, I do not look forward to leaving my chief for school. I feel sometimes as if I am an outline of myself, and each thing I learn from him is like a colored piece of yarn that gets knitted inside that outline, filling me, making me more defined. The longer I work with Mr. Soper, the more a pattern of him knits into me. He has become such an important, inseparable part of my whole being.

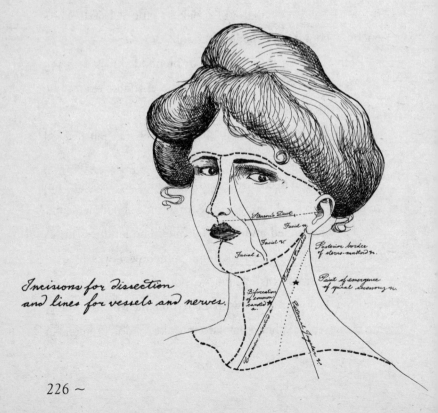

Incisions for dissection and lines for vessels and nerves.

March 6, 1907

These books Dr. Baker gave me are different, not dull or dusty like Latin texts, but full of fascinating stories. All day I carry the one I'm reading on Dr. Louis Pasteur, and open it whenever I have a spare moment.

He was the first to prove the germ theory.

It used to be thought that disease was caused by something outside of ourselves, like clouds of bad odors, or something inside ourselves, like the four humors (blood, phlegm, yellow bile, and black bile).

Dr. Pasteur had the radical idea that something *alive* was *feeding* on us, and *that* was making us sick. He got the notion from observing grapes fermenting into wine, and then souring. He examined the ruined wine under the microscope and discovered that there were creatures living in it. Germs, bacteria. He found them everywhere—in the water and food that humans consumed, in our bodies—and his brain made a great leap. He connected these germs to the ones that were making people ill.

I think of the lambs on Anushka's farm, the three sickly ones with runny eyes and sores in their mouths, and then I think of Dr. Pasteur, of the sheep he saved. He watched them die of anthrax and knew he had to help them.

He applied his germ theory to the sheep. He removed the anthrax germs from them, killed them, and injected the dead germs into healthy sheep, making their bodies accustomed to the disease, and so immune to it.

It's a brilliant mind that can even imagine such things as bacteria. Doing these experiments, how did he know what to look for? When he saw the wine, what made him think there might be something alive in there? How did he make the connection between wine and anthrax?

I wish I had the ability, as Dr. Baker described, to see the larger picture. Even more than that, I wish I could make leaps and see things that the rest of the world doesn't see. Perhaps I will one day, once I've studied everything.

I must push myself to think harder.

salmonella typhi bacteria

March 7, 1907

What occurred this morning has altered me in a way I cannot reconcile. I have not spoken to anybody about it, and am not sure how I ever will.

A stranger came into our office today. At first I thought it was another reporter who somehow got past the police guards and was hunting me down for more details on the Mary Mallon case. It turned out the man had read my name in the newspaper and came with a secret that he'd been holding on to for nearly a decade.

For some reason, I don't know why, I feared his presence the moment I saw him. Whatever news this man had to offer, Mr. Soper would hear, but I could not stop him from taking the chair across from me, and I certainly could not ask Mr. Soper to leave.

He said his name was Tim Wilcox. He was missing his

right leg and walked with canes. His clothes hung loosely from his thin chest, his eyes seemed ill and watery as he stared at me.

"You look just like him," he said quietly.

"To whom are you referring, sir?" I asked.

He handed over a large coin on a chain, though it didn't seem like a regular coin.

"Your father. That's where I met him," he said, pointing to the coin.

All the breath in my body left me. I shook my head. My mind was suddenly blank. "I'm sorry, I don't understand," I said.

"That's his war badge," Mr. Wilcox said. He tapped a cane against his good leg. "After the Spanish blew up the USS *Maine* docked in the Cuban harbor, me and your father were sent to fight alongside Roosevelt."

My face felt numb, my mouth dry. I looked more closely at the badge, the imprint of the American flag, and the name stamped on it. I ran my finger over the letters, GREGORY GALEWSKI, ARMY ID NUMBER 3040. My father's name.

I looked up at the man. Words blocked my throat, the question at my lips.

Is he alive?

"We were overcome by land forces on the beach," Mr. Wilcox went on. "I was shot in the thigh and your father carried me into the forest, to our headquarters, where they removed my leg. As you can see, I recovered. Not all of me, but enough."

He took a deep breath.

"I'm sorry I can't say the same for your pa," he said.

It couldn't be! I stared at the man, trying to understand, trying not to believe him. I coughed and shook my head, swallowing back tears. We've waited so long, hoping for his return, and now this!

I looked over at Mr. Soper. When I met his eyes, he stood and excused himself from the room, saying he had to see Mr. Briggs. I wanted to reach for him, but he slipped away.

The man gestured to the badge in my hand. "Your father asked me to keep that from the medical doctors, to hide his badge so he would not be counted among the dead," he said.

"But why?" I whispered.

"He was sick with the yellow fever. He wanted you to remember him . . . in a certain way. He wanted you to think he was shot, or taken hostage, he said. Not killed by disease."

My father seemed cruel to me suddenly, cruel in his

desire to maintain his honor. Pride, it was blind pride that made him do it.

"He wanted me to go to my grave with his secret, but then I saw your name in the paper," Mr. Wilcox said. "With me not so far from my own grave, it wasn't right. I thought you should know."

I closed my eyes, grateful that this man had come to me. My heart ached, but I knew the truth.

I put the badge on my desk, looking at my father's name. This piece of metal had hung around his neck. He had touched this man in front of me, he had saved his life.

"Did—did he ever speak of me?" I asked. My voice sounded high and weak.

Mr. Wilcox nodded. "You and your mother. And your brother, his son, Benjamin."

He shook his head sadly.

"Miss Galewski, I want you to know I argued with your pa about his decision. But he was a stubborn ox and wouldn't listen. Since he saved my life, I had to respect his wishes. Up till now, of course. I hope I did the right thing."

I looked into his watery eyes; I wanted to reach over my desk and touch him, to bring back my father through him. I laced my fingers and squeezed them together as hard as I could.

"Of course you did the right thing," I said. "Thank you, Mr. Wilcox. If you hadn't come, we would never have known. We've waited so long."

I could not help the cry that escaped from me, the tears that streamed down my face. I covered my eyes with my hands, pushing back the flood that tumbled out of me. I couldn't stop it. Mr. Wilcox cleared his throat. He said my name. I looked up and saw him standing before my desk, holding out a handkerchief. I took it. He bowed his head and limped to the door and quietly left.

I felt as if my insides had collapsed. How would I tell Marm? How would she feel? And how could my father have been so selfish? Didn't he know how much we loved him? Did he think we would forget him? Not wait for him? All the years, all the sorrow we bottled up, all the hope that's kept us going—how could he have done this to us?

I heard footsteps outside the door and hastily wiped the tears from my face. I slid the badge from the desk and put it in the drawer where I also kept the few brief notes Mr. Soper had written to me. I had to focus on my work. I had to find a way to keep going. I opened a case folio and rolled a piece of paper into the typing machine. I placed my fingers on the keys and made myself move them.

Mr. Soper returned. He sat at his desk and went to work without addressing me. I was relieved by his silent presence beside me. I don't know how I lasted out the day, but somehow I did.

When work finished this evening, I removed the badge and the notes from the drawer and fit them into my purse. Mr. Soper left the building with me and walked me to the streetcar stop. There, he took my hand. "I'm sorry for your loss," he said.

His touch reached straight into me. The warmth of his hand soothed my shocked heart.

"Mr. Soper," I said, "I apologize for not telling you—"

"You were being very professional, Prudence, and I appreciate that."

He still held my hand. He was so near, I could smell his sweet cologne.

"For years we did not know what had become of my father," I said.

Mr. Soper took my other hand.

"It's difficult to lose a loved one," he said. "You're a brave girl."

His brown eyes looked into mine. The blood beat in my ears. My face burned. He released my hands just as my trolley pulled in and opened its doors. And then, I did the unthinkable. I felt he would not turn me away. I rose up and kissed him on the cheek. Then I ran up the steps without bidding him good night. On the streetcar, I could feel the roughness of his skin, the edge of his mustache on my lips. I can feel it still. I berated myself for not being able to contain my feelings.

I came home to an empty, cold house. A note from Marm told me she was at a birth. I started a fire in the stove and tried to push away the persistent question that nagged at me: What had I just done? The prospect of facing Mr. Soper suddenly frightened me.

I splashed my face with cool water from the basin. I took the badge and my chief's precious notes and hid them inside my blotter case by the window. Then I began to scrub potatoes for stew.

At last Marm came home, blood on her skirt, a sadness hanging about her. Sensing that the birth had not gone well, I hesitated telling her of the visit. All evening I tried to think of a way to break the news. But Marm seemed too tired and sad.

I write this now, unable to sleep. Beside me, I hold the book Papa gave me—after Benny died and he left, it was the one thing that kept my hope strong, that he would come back, and I could talk to him about all that I had learned from it.

And now, to find that a disease has taken his life . . .

After Papa left, something in me cracked and leaked one drop at a time. With the news this stranger brought, a giant gush has broken through the crack, and all the water has poured out. Now I am left with a vast hollowness that I know not how to fill.

March 8, 1907

In all the years I waited for him, I didn't allow myself to think he would never come back. I thought I would not survive the news of his death, but I woke in the dark and felt my own heart beating.

Yet the world around me has changed somehow. It is a world without Papa.

Unable to sleep any longer, I got up and walked to work, my toes nearly freezing in my boots. When I arrived at our building, I found that my feet, cold as they were, would not allow me to go in. I could not face my chief's knowing eyes, the closeness of him. I walked three times around the block before the obligation of work overwhelmed me.

At the front door of our building, I felt my chief just behind me and turned.

He nodded stiffly at me and said, "Good morning, Prudence."

"Good morning, sir," I said.

He reached ahead of me and pulled the door open for me. I went inside; he kept pace just behind me, until we got to our office, which he unlocked. He turned the gas key, lighting the lights.

We sat at our respective desks.

I waited for him to chastise me, or to say something about my father, but he said nothing.

I organized the bottom drawer of my desk. I rearranged my pencils and quills. I changed the paper on my blotter pad and filled all my ink bottles.

He left the office for a meeting with Mr. Briggs. Around midday, he returned and stood before my desk and said my name. He held up a folio.

"I have notes of a new case," he said. "Several children have fallen ill with the typhoid in Riverdale."

I reached over my desk for the notes. My fingers accidentally brushed his when I took the folio. It felt like putting my hand into a flame.

"I will type them up right away, sir," I said.

"That's fine," he said.

I could not wait for this day to end.

March 10, 1907

I have not yet told Marm about Papa. I'm not sure what I'm waiting for. I wished so completely for his return these past nine years, and now all I can feel is his absence.

Telling Marm would allow her the chance to begin anew, but something in me wants to hold the information to myself just a little longer. It's as if this knowledge has brought a strange circle of fate upon me—I cannot help but think of Mary Mallon, and the fever she carries within her. I think of my father's death by yellow fever. It seems Mary brought me to Papa somehow. To solve something, the crime of disease.

There's one image of him that comes repeatedly to me. The day after Benny died, my father said the Kaddish in his memory. He spoke it in Hebrew, along with Rabbi Samsfield. I hear the intonations of the prayer like a whisper in my mind all the time now.

I read last night that two of Louis Pasteur's children died of typhoid.

Marm was married to Papa for seventeen years before he left, and another nine of waiting. That is a long time to have someone in your heart.

I feel as if I'm traveling through a dark tunnel. Once I reach the other side, I will have the strength to break the news to her.

March 14, 1907

Mr. Soper is not himself with me; he places obstacles in our path, people and projects, and I wish I knew my way back into his good graces.

For the second time, Jonathan, that strange science fellow, has come to my aid. I fear that Mr. Soper may be encouraging him to make friends with me. Everyone in the department now knows that I'm studying for the medical school entrance examination—the science fellows question me when they see me in the hall, and not always in the nicest manner. This morning a boy heckled me about animal reproduction, and Jonathan came along and grabbed the boy by his neck and pushed him on. He then turned and apologized to me for his friend's behavior. I don't know what impression he thinks this made on me.

That wasn't the only exchange. Later Jonathan came

into the office, greeted Mr. Soper, and placed a medical journal on my desk. "You'll find the article on page forty-nine helpful to your case," he said, with a big, open smile. Mr. Soper and Jonathan nodded to each other as the boy left. Mr. Soper didn't give me the article himself directly—yet he knows the difficulty I had with Jonathan.

It's been harder, spending days in the office with my chief. I fear his dismissal of me.

I quickly read the article the boy gave me. It illustrated how white blood cells engulf and devour any invading bacteria, and how, in a healthy body, this creates a natural immunity to sickness. I tried to speak with Mr. Soper about it, but the darkness around his brow showed me the painful doubt that he entertained about me.

"I'm glad that—that young man—gave me this to read," I started.

My chief met my eyes for the barest of seconds. "Yes," he said, "Jonathan. He's quite a brilliant young science fellow; he's always finding the most pertinent journal reports."

This description hit me hard. I would say Dr. Pasteur is brilliant, or Dr. Mechnikov, but not that simple boy.

I asked, "Do you think this might explain how Mary can carry disease while being immune to it?"

Mr. Soper ran his finger down a column of figures distractedly. "It could," he said.

"We have not heard back from the island doctors about Mary's problematic gallbladder, have we?" I asked.

He looked up and sighed. "When we do, I expect it will explain a lot, Miss Galewski."

The way he said it troubled me deeply.

Mr. Soper and I have shared so many discussions about cells and disease. He gave me my first glimpse under the microscope. He taught me how to read charts and reports, and how to write them. I am sickened with worry that he now sees me as an unserious, flighty thing. I must endure; I must make a great effort to earn back his respect.

March 15, 1907

I took out the very first red silk tablet I ever wrote in. The beginning date was January 2, 1900, two years after Papa left us. He was not yet officially missing.

I was a different girl then. I still smelled the metal on his hands from the factory, I still heard the timbre of his voice in my chest when he spoke. I could feel his rough hair against my cheek when he kissed me. I heard him calling my name from our window, calling me and Benny inside to light the Shabbat candles.

I cried alone, reading the words of my childish self, emptying my eyes of the tears I'd held on to for all his missing years. I sobbed until my chest ached. I hugged my quilt to me like gauze to a wound for a long time, long enough to stop the bleeding.

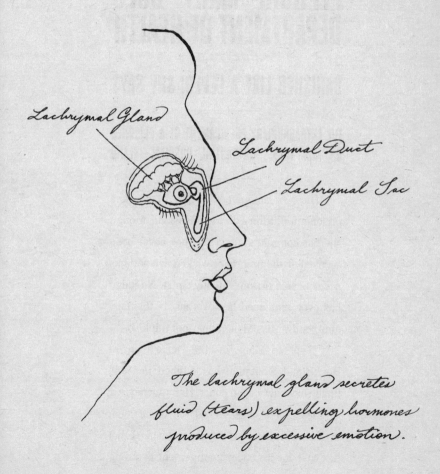

Lachrymal Gland

Lachrymal Duct

Lachrymal Sac

The lachrymal gland secretes
fluid (tears) expelling hormones
produced by excessive emotion.

The New York American

MARCH 16, 1907   FIVE CENTS

TYPHOID MARY SUES DEPARTMENT OF HEALTH

BANISHED LIKE A LEPER! SHE SAYS

THE EXTRAORDINARY PREDICAMENT OF A PRISONER ON NEW YORK'S QUARANTINE HOSPITAL ISLAND

The now-famous cook Mary Mallon is a prisoner for life on a quarantine island, though she has committed no crime, has never been accused of an immoral or wicked act, and has never been a prisoner in any court. No judge has ever sentenced her. We ask, is this fair? Apparently, Miss Mallon does not think so.

"Typhoid Mary," as the Department of Health and Sanitation has dubbed her, will finally have her day in court. Her attorney, Mr. Charles O'Neal, has served the department with a writ of habeas corpus. He states that her case for improper confinement is strong,

and that if the judge is fair and reasonable, she should be a freed woman in short order. Mary Mallon has been in captivity for nearly three months, since January, when she was imprisoned for being a human culture tube for the typhoid germ.

In a letter written for the court, Miss Mallon claims, "I have never had typhoid in my life, nor do I have it now. Why should I be banished like a leper and forced to live in solitary confinement? My own doctors say I have no typhoid germs. I am an innocent human being. I have committed no crime and I am

Deadly

treated like an outcast—a criminal. It is unjust, outrageous, uncivilized. It seems incredible that in a Christian community a defenseless woman can be treated in this manner."

Mary Mallon, who is physically healthy in every way, is being kept on a quarantine island just north of New York City, along with dozens of consumptives, recovering and otherwise. The department has not answered questions as to how they maintain her good health on such an island, nor when she might be released. They have appealed to eminent lawyers on the question of legality concerning Miss Mallon's confinement, and insist a judge will see that "Typhoid Mary" is a menace to society. They claim that she should be kept contained indefinitely.

———————

March 20, 1907

It seems impossible that the newspapers could sink any lower, but they have. This illustration horrifies me, as does the name they have invented for Mary. They have taken her up as a sport—they toss around her name and her image like a tennis ball. There is nothing anyone can do to control them.

What's worse, this article contains a good deal of fact.

It turns out that the nurses on the island have been assisting in Mary's case, acting as messengers to bring her feces to an independent laboratory in Manhattan. Apparently, this laboratory has *not* found typhoid. Several weeks of independent testing on Mary's samples have been done, and each has come out clean. I don't understand the methods they use; Mr. Soper says the samples must be old, or the laboratory must be bad. Who knows if they are even

Mary's samples? On top of the insult of Mr. O'Neal taking us to court, Mr. Soper is doubly upset by this so-called proof that Mary's lawyer aims to present.

We believe the Bowing family is involved in retaining such a bulldog of a lawyer, though they have managed to keep their name out of it. Instead of dragging the case through the court system, Mr. O'Neal has served the department with a writ of habeas corpus, which allows a prisoner who feels he or she is unfairly imprisoned court time with a judge. Without a jury, a judge alone will decide Mary's case. He can do this in one day of hearing if he wants. And if he decides that the department is wrong to have captured her, he can free her immediately.

In our defense, our scientists are gathering evidence for the phenomenon of a healthy carrier. They have simplified Dr. Koch's seminal text on his initial discovery of the first German who spread typhoid unknowingly through his feces. They're also translating Dr. Mechnikov's work on white blood cells and immunity, and Dr. Pasteur's study of the life of bacteria inside the human body. I've spent the past few days retyping the first of these papers, which has been an education in itself. I hope a judge will not be swayed by Mr. Bowing's influence at the mayor's office, but rather that he will take the time to read these important papers and understand our position.

Our attorneys are discussing the legal rights of the department, and which law is stronger—a person's right to freedom, or the public's right to a healthy, protected community. There is a law (Section 1170) that states that the Board of Health and Sanitation of the City of New York may remove from the public arena *any* person sick with *any* contagious, pestilential, or infectious disease. It seems clear, yet one question stumps these smart men: Can Mary legally be defined as a person *sick* with an infectious disease?

For the next weeks until the trial, I fear we will be on pins and needles. There's been an outbreak of typhoid in Riverdale, which Mr. Soper suspects may be caused by another healthy carrier like Mary. If we can uncover another example, perhaps that will strengthen our case. It makes sense to me that Mary is not an exception, but rather part of a larger invisible problem that must be addressed.

As an experiment, Mr. Soper asked the science fellows to test several people in the department who have survived the typhoid fever. We have discovered that they do *not* carry the typhoid germ. So it proves that not everyone who has had the fever automatically falls into the category of healthy carrier. Mr. Soper says he thinks that most people survive the fever without continuing to produce the germ. Indeed, we have not found another like Mary. Do they exist? And if so, must we test every single survivor in order to find out whether they carry the germ?

Tomorrow we are to travel to Riverdale to begin investigating the new typhoid outbreak. I'm anxious to discover the reason for this epidemic. It seems similar in some respects to the Thompson case, with clusters of people falling ill as if from a tainted source rather than a contagion.

After reading about Dr. Pasteur's work, a strange thing now happens to me when I travel with crowds of people in a public streetcar or omnibus. I see them as a myriad of undetected illnesses. Sicknesses we don't yet know, ones we can't yet diagnose. My eye picks out the weaker-looking ones, and I see the bacteria, as varied and crowded as a metropolis, living within them.

I see my future work in those people.

March 30, 1907

Our trips to Riverdale have opened up a disturbing realm of inquiry for us and have added another dimension to Mary's case.

Mr. Soper and I took a train and carriage up to the Bronx to investigate. We discovered records of typhoid fever in this part of Riverdale dating as far back as November of last year. All together, the count was ninety-six people ill, thirteen dead—and news of more victims coming in every day. A horrifyingly large number of people.

We went to the hospital to visit the latest cases, hoping to get the freshest information possible. We visited seven patients. One, a girl of eight years, kept running to the toilet. Another child could barely sit up for the pain in her head. We spoke to both of their mothers and obtained useful information from them. We then moved on to a poor fellow who was raving something about his neighbor's wife, but he was too deep into dementia and too close to death to interview. Four women had the same rose-shaped rashes that had appeared on Amy Thompson, but they were able to talk, and answered our questions about what they ate and where they shopped and who they had encountered in the past month. That, and the mothers' interviews, was enough to give us our answer.

All the victims had bought their milk, butter, and cream at Kinley's Farm. We wasted no time in going over there and took several samples to be tested. All of the milk was clean, as was the cream, but a batch of the butter turned out to be positive for the typhoid.

We returned to the farm, bringing with us Dr. Baker and Jonathan so we could test the farmer and several of his farmhands on the spot. The doctor convinced them of the quotidian nature of the test and drew blood from each person, and the boy performed the Widal blood serum test on the samples. All of them came out negative except Mr. Kinley's.

The man is rife with typhoid germs.

Imagine our surprise to find a second healthy carrier, and so quickly! Though Mr. Kinley doesn't do the milking on a regular basis, occasionally he pitches in. But he is the only one who forms the butter into slabs, and he does this with his bare hands. This is how he transmits the fever.

Mr. Kinley had heard about Mary Mallon, who he referred to as Typhoid Mary, which unfortunately I hear very often now. He laughed about the filthy Irish—until he understood the results of his own Widal test. Mr. Soper pointed out the epidemic in Riverdale. Mr. Kinley denied that he was to blame for it; his fury made me fear things would turn ugly. Dr. Baker firmly reminded him of the police intervention in Miss Mallon's case, and the farmer reluctantly agreed to accompany us back to the Detention Hospital, where he remains in quarantine.

This is a very disquieting discovery. I don't think anyone had truly envisioned another healthy carrier would exist, except Mr. Soper, who seemed to know it all along. There has been a great outcry that Mr. Kinley was not simply tested and released, but is now being held in detention. There have been many letters to the papers, and his wife is very upset. The reporters scream that soon we will have every other healthy New Yorker in quarantine, and for no good reason. No member of the press has bothered to travel to the Memorial Hospital in Riverdale to visit those children and men and women who burn with fever and clutch at their bellies in pain thanks to the salmonella typhi bacteria that Mr. Kinley unknowingly passed to them. If they did, they would see the truth. They would see the reason we keep him from the public. They wouldn't defend the germ over the man.

I'm beginning to see that it takes a certain endurance to make unpopular decisions. I suppose this is one of the more difficult challenges a doctor has to face. I don't yet know what the department plans to do with Mr. Kinley. Perhaps it depends on the judge's decision in Mary's case. We don't know how many of these healthy carriers exist, nor what causes them, nor what to do about them. There simply is no precedent for any of this.

Mr. Soper seems to be including Jonathan in every aspect of our case now. The young man's involvement pains me. He is to appear at Mary's hearing, along with several scientists from his department. Out of all the science fellows, why him?

Perhaps I am to have compassion for Jonathan. I overheard him and Dr. Baker speaking on the train. He grew up in the St. Francis Orphanage after his parents died. He was too young to know them. He has no brothers or sisters. All of this seemed to bring out the deepest pity in Dr. Baker. He has survived many difficulties, a life of crime and vice on the streets, and overcame them. He comes from another world, but it's one that seems too far from my own to understand.

April 6, 1907

The case is moving so fast, I have hardly enough time to keep up with my notes here. Eleven of us are scheduled to appear before the judge: Mr. Soper and I, Dr. Baker and the two officers, Jonathan, three senior scientists, Dr. Parks, and a doctor from the island. We gathered in the lecture room, and the lawyers talked us through their plan for the defense—a straight line leading from the disease to Mary.

They told us what they thought Mary's lawyer Mr. O'Neal might say, and what questions we might be asked on cross-examination. They suggested we think about what is truth, and what will win the case. They said to use phrases that will stress Mary's obstinacy and violent uncooperativeness.

As the time approaches, the idea of speaking before a judge frightens me more and more—especially when I have been advised to see the truth as selectable, rather than as a whole. I'm not even sure I know what that means, really. Can't we simply tell the whole story and let the judge decide? Won't truth prevail?

Oh, I wish I was not called to appear in court!

April 8, 1907

One week before I see Mary Mallon in the flesh again, and the thought makes the nerves in my stomach buzz. I fear she will point to me in the courtroom and scream out "You!" as she did in my nightmare.

I walk around with this raw, uncomfortable sense of being revealed. I cannot rid myself of this horrible feeling.

We had another meeting with the lawyers in which they arranged our placement before the judge. In the courtroom, I will sit between Mr. Soper and Dr. Baker in the first row, with Jonathan and the scientists directly behind us. At this meeting, Jonathan kept reaching forward and tapping me on the shoulder to tell me something, but I gracefully deflected his attempts at conversation.

I did not know anyone was watching me do this.

When the meeting concluded, Dr. Baker leaned over

and asked me to join her in her office. Something about her request, the gravity in her eyes, worried me. I asked if we were to begin our tutoring, but she shook her head and held up her hand to stop any other questions.

I followed her upstairs to her office, where she waved me into a chair as she settled into hers. She leaned her elbows on the desk and folded her hands and rested her chin on them, as if she were searching for the right words.

"Prudence," she started, "I'm not sure there is any good way to discuss this, other than to be blunt and come right out with it."

"Please do," I said.

"It's important that our department work together in harmony," she said.

"Of course," I said. I tried to see in her eyes what she was thinking, but she was inscrutable.

"It's also important that you as a woman get along with your male colleagues. You might as well start now, because you don't know who will be helpful to you in the future."

I did not picture myself as someone who didn't get along with others. I said I was surprised she had seen that in me.

"I sense some discord between you and Jonathan," she said.

My mind raced back to the morning he trapped me. My tongue felt pasted to the roof of my mouth.

"I hear him trying to be cordial to you, but you are almost rude to him," she went on.

I looked at Dr. Baker's lovely face and wondered if she had ever had difficulties with men.

"He's an intelligent young man, and by the looks of his clever experiments in our laboratory, I can see he will make a powerful scientist one day. Those are the sort of men who can influence your career," she said.

"It's that—I just—Ma'am, I'm not sure that boy will ever respect me as a doctor," I stammered.

She frowned. "What do you mean?" she asked.

Something in her voice made me feel I could trust her and confess what happened. I took a deep breath and told her about that morning, how the boy tried to kiss me, how Mr. Soper saved me. Her lips turned white with anger while I spoke.

She closed her eyes for a long moment, then opened them, looking straight into mine. "It will happen, Prudence," she said. "There is a lot of ignorance among men, so you must teach them how to treat you. By ignoring Jonathan, you're not furthering your relations. You must be better than him, smarter than him."

In her cool eyes, I saw the steeliness inside her—that hard place that allowed her to barge into strange houses and wrestle down disease. It was a place of pure resolve.

"You must be careful with your emotions," she went on. "You mustn't allow your dislike of one man, or your love for another"—she lightly stressed the word "love" without looking at me—"to interfere with your work and your studies. You must learn to stay neutral. Save your passion for yourself and the knowledge you must acquire," she said.

Her words revealed me; I felt bared before her. She knew my feelings for Mr. Soper! She released me, and as I walked down the stairs, it occurred to me that she wasn't the only one who could see my feelings so clearly. Mr. Soper had not returned to his previous kind self since I had kissed him. He was civil and straightforward, professional, but no longer openly kind.

Had he spoken to Dr. Baker about me?

Had other people noticed?

I worried that everyone in the department saw right into my secret heart. I feared they all knew my mash on Mr. Soper, and my dislike for Jonathan.

When I reached our office, I said a brief good night to Mr. Soper and left. I did not take the streetcar, but walked the mile home. I have been thinking about what Dr. Baker said. She has learned to be careful with her emotions, to see men as influencing her career, as stepping stones to a future goal. Has she ever felt raw and revealed? Has she ever loved?

I am afraid perhaps she sees me the way I see Josephine—irrational, excitable, susceptible to the ways of men. I'm afraid she thinks she made the wrong decision about me when she chose to help me with medical school. If only I could rid myself of this anguish. I must learn to speak to people in a cool, controlled manner. Oh, how the weight of my own self presses me to earth! I wish I could hold my breath and sink down deep into the East River and feel the water flow over me, taking away the tide of my emotions.

April 10, 1907

I wish I could speak to Marm about Papa, but I know he lives inside her every moment of every day, that she thinks of him upon rising in the morning, and nights before bed. I don't want her to suffer the fate of knowing that he will never return.

I wonder if Papa himself had this thought. If that's why he didn't want us to find out.

Keeping the knowledge inside me is like holding a knife in my chest. No matter what I try to do to avoid it, still, the pain is there.

I must find a way to tell her.

April 14, 1907

The trial began today. I cannot blame my blunder in the courtroom on anyone but myself. Yet I feel Mr. Soper should have known what might happen. He should have known and warned me somehow.

This morning, as I walked through a light drizzle to the courthouse near the Brooklyn Bridge, I felt weary from a nervous sleep. When I came within view of the huge stone building, I saw a group of women at the bottom of the wide stairway with a banner that said FREE MARY MALLON! Bunches of angry people held signs that said IF SHE'S TYPHOID MARY, THEN I'M DIPHTHERIA DAN! and RELEASE FARMER KINLEY NOW! They furiously shouted their slogans. I felt like they were shouting at me.

At the top of the steps, Dr. Baker stood between two great columns, talking to Jonathan.

Men with cameras and press hats took pictures of the protesters. The courtroom, and our case, was ordered closed to reporters by the judge. My heart thumped harder as I wove through the crowd, up the stairs to the doctor. I forced myself to meet Jonathan's eyes and say "Good morning," a greeting that he returned. I stood beside him as we waited for Mr. Soper, who darted between two carriages and came toward us, studiously ignoring the crowd.

As Mr. Soper took the last few steps, Jonathan opened the door to the courthouse and we all went inside. We walked through the marble halls until we found the proper room, a muffled, wood-paneled square with rows of pews like a synagogue, and a high podium for the judge.

We took our seats behind our lawyers; others gathered, until the courtroom held the witnesses that would be called on both sides. I saw the Thompsons, and the Bowings, and other families who had hired Mary Mallon. Jonathan pointed out Mr. O'Neal, Mary's lawyer, and two of the men who sat behind him. He said, "They're the independent scientists who say she doesn't carry the germ. Lab rats!"

Outside the room, I could hear the voices of men, reporters waiting for Mary to appear, which she did shortly, but through a door in front, accompanied by a nurse and a policeman. The room fell silent. She was well coiffed, her collar starched, her dress clean and pressed. She seemed heavier; she didn't look at any of us; she sat beside her lawyer and gripped the arms of her chair. Something in my chest squeezed tight, looking at her—this woman whose whole life had changed because of what she carried around inside her. She had become an idea in my head, a germ theory, but there she sat, flesh and bone, and that bad, tight feeling moved all through me.

The judge entered and sat, and the lawyers stated their cases—Mary Mallon versus the Department of Health and Sanitation. The first witness called was Mr. Soper, who went through the story of how we had discovered that Mary was a healthy carrier of the typhoid disease. He seemed very dignified on the stand and kept to the basic scientific data that was detailed in the folios I'd written of the case. He was questioned for about twenty minutes, and cross-questioned for another fifteen, and then it was my turn.

I tried to appear as calm as my chief. I repeated much of what Mr. Soper said, telling how I kept notes and followed the food trail to the peach ice cream, which led us to Miss Mallon. But on cross-questioning, Mr. O'Neal asked me things other than what he had asked Mr. Soper.

I didn't understand where he was going until it was too late.

"And how did you find out where Mary Mallon lived?" Mr. O'Neal asked.

"Mr. Soper and I waited outside the house where she worked," I said. "I was away for Christmas, and when I came back, we went to a saloon and talked to a man about her, who agreed to set up a meeting with her."

"How did you get the man to agree to this?" the lawyer asked.

I saw my mistake then—the rummy sat in the pew behind Mr. O'Neal, and I knew he had told of the monetary exchange. O'Neal brought me right to the confession.

"We—we offered him a few dollars."

"You bribed him?" Mr. O'Neal asked. "You spied on Mary, followed her, and bribed her friend? Is that normal protocol for the Department of Health and Sanitation? Spying and bribing?"

Our lawyers objected to O'Neal's translation of our actions, but the judge allowed the question.

I glanced at the judge, whose bushy gray brows shaded his eyes. He waited for the answer; they all did. I felt my mouth open, a hundred words clinging to the back of my tongue. I found in the crowd Mr. Soper's agonized brown eyes. I felt a great flood of anger toward him then—for leading me to this, for not warning me.

Then I understood what our lawyers had said: In order to keep Mary from cooking for the public, we must explain her stubborn resistance.

"She was violent when we tried to approach her properly," I said. "She screamed and brandished a knife at us. She threw a cooking fork at us. She curses us and doesn't believe us, and that's why she's dangerous to—"

O'Neal stopped me. "That's all, Miss Galewski," he said. "You are excused. You may step down now."

I looked at our lawyers' stricken eyes as I returned to my seat. My row was filled with fallen faces; only Mr. Soper met my eyes. My cheeks burned with embarrassment, tears blurred my vision. Even Jonathan seemed disappointed. Why hadn't O'Neal asked Mr. Soper these questions? Why didn't our lawyers warn me? But I knew—I had not written of the spying or the bribe in my office notes; our lawyers weren't aware of Mr. Soper's methods. But he should've known. I sat beside my chief and looked at the back of Mary's bunned head. I prayed she would not be freed on account of Mr. Soper's irregular ways of obtaining information. On account of my own blunder in confessing them.

Dr. Baker was called to the stand next, and I made myself listen to her testimony over the hum of distress in my head. She too was put to the test when asked about her decision to enter the house without a warrant, but she handled it with a cold sureness, stating the department's policies, and our goal to remove the evil of disease from the public sphere in any manner possible, whether the disease be water, or food, or a human carrier.

"The urgency was upon us," she said firmly.

"You could not take an extra day to obtain a proper warrant from this court?" O'Neal asked.

"No, we certainly could not," she said. "A day could mean another person's illness. We didn't want to risk that."

Her conviction fortified me. I vowed to myself that one day, I would be as strong as she.

Once O'Neal finished with her, a scientist was called. He talked about bacteria and the carriage of germs. He handed the judge all the papers he and the others had written. On cross, O'Neal asked the man if the theory of a healthy carrier was officially accepted by the Academy of Medicine, and the scientist had to conclude that it was not.

Jonathan was called next. He gave a short lecture on the Widal test, and how Mary's samples to the independent laboratory were only feces, and not as definite as the blood test.

"When feces are not fresh, the typhoid germ dies, and the test shows as negative," he said. "If you'd allow me to give her a Widal test right now, I could show you that she is positive. Mary is a dangerous carrier."

"That will not be necessary," Mr. O'Neal replied.

"A blood test is the only way to be sure," Jonathan went on. He talked about Mr. Kinley, our second healthy carrier, and I saw the judge's eyes open wider with interest. Jonathan managed to tell most of the Riverdale story, the extent of that epidemic caused by our second healthy carrier, before O'Neal insisted he leave the stand.

The day concluded with testimony from Dr. Parks, who stated that he believed Mary carried the typhoid in her gallbladder. The judge agreed to continue the hearing until all the witnesses were called, which could take another week.

I left the courtroom, anxious to escape home, aware of Mr. Soper keeping pace beside me. On the street, we were instantly surrounded by the press and public wanting to know what had happened. My chief touched my shoulder; he met my eyes and nodded; I followed close behind as he led the way through the crowd without giving them a statement.

Once we were clear of the mob, I said, "I could not help it."

He walked with his hands behind his back, his head bent in thought. "No, it's not your fault, Prudence," he said.

He seemed older and weaker to me suddenly, tired of fighting this never-ending battle against the media and Mary, who refused to understand that she carried disease.

"That lawyer is a nasty piece of business," Mr. Soper said, "and you handled him well."

The secret tasks we had performed bound us together. I saw that, and I felt able to forgive him.

I felt, as well, a certain forgiveness from him.

We walked across town in silence, our human failings a sort of truce between us.

April 15, 1907

I did not mean for Marm to find out about Papa this way. I wish I had told her sooner. I wish I didn't have such bad news.

After another day of listening to testimony, I reached home and found Marm standing in the front room, holding my blotter case, staring down at the table.

Spread there were my father's war badge and the notes from Mr. Soper.

My stomach tightened. I could see she had stumbled upon the badge and notes by accident. Her face seemed a strange shape to me, triangular, with twisted lines along her cheeks. I had come home wanting to speak to her about the court case, which we had not yet discussed. I was not prepared to encounter her this way. The air around her seemed colored a bright blue, so thick I felt as if I could hardly walk into the room. I wondered how long she had been standing there, waiting for me.

When she lifted her eyes, blue air came at me like a wave.

She picked up the war badge and held it in her palm. "Where did this come from?"

"A man named Mr. Wilcox saw my name in the paper," I said quickly. "He knew Papa in the war; they fought together; Papa saved his life. Then he died. I'm sorry, Marm, I was going to tell you. Papa died of the yellow fever a long time ago. He didn't want us to know, so he gave his badge to Mr. Wilcox."

I felt the knife in my chest come loose.

Marm moaned, closing her fingers over the badge. Her hand trembled. "His father died in the Civil War that way," she whispered. She laughed bitterly, wiping her tears angrily from her eyes. "He was no hero defending a hill. He died of smallpox. Your father never forgave him that."

She shook her head and held her breath to stop a sob. I counted the seconds—smallpox, smallpox, smallpox.

"Your father and I argued over this, his brave idea to join the army. I didn't want him to go." She shook her head, and it all came tumbling out: "When Benny's leg turned to gangrene, your father quit his job at the factory to take care of him. I had started my apprenticeship with Granny Rosa by then, and my time was unpredictable. I was afraid your father would lose his job; I wanted to put Benny in the public infirmary, but he wouldn't hear of it. He watched over that boy day and night, carrying him out to the street for fresh air. And when he died, your father tried to go back to work, but they wouldn't let him into the factory. No one else would hire him. They couldn't trust a man who would leave his job for a child. We had no money, we started fighting—those terrible fights."

She put her hand to her forehead as if to keep the memories from invading.

Nine years, we waited.

A lifetime.

She dropped the badge on the table and went into the back room. I didn't know if she went to cry, or if she would return. I heard her moving around, and I dragged the badge slowly along the surface of the table on its chain. I wondered if she had read the notes from Mr. Soper; they sat open, five of them, like pages of a half-read newspaper.

Papa meant to come back. He had left to make money, he intended to come back.

Marm reappeared with a framed picture in her hand. In

it, a sturdy young man in a sharp black suit gripped the hand of a smiling girl in a white dress. I stared at his face: dark circles under piercing black eyes, cheeks narrow and long, mouth set in a triumphant line. They stood in front of a loopy roller coaster, and I knew the sound of the ocean roared in their ears—they'd just gotten married in Coney Island.

"We met on a bench at the beach," Marm said. "I was fifteen and he was seventeen and he sat himself down right next to me and asked me if I'd ever eaten raw oysters. I said I had not, and Gregory disappeared. I looked around for my aunt, who was my chaperone for the day. On a bench, under her parasol, was Aunt Gertrude, fast asleep."

Marm began to laugh at the memory. She dabbed at the tears in her eyes with the tips of her fingers and sighed. I smiled; Marm leaned over and cupped my cheek with her hand.

"Your father returned a few moments later with a plate of raw oysters," she said.

"Did you eat them?" I asked.

She wrinkled her nose and nodded. "I didn't want to insult your father," she said. "They were from his cousin Schmuel, who ran an oyster bar that wasn't very kosher and went bankrupt. Schmuel went to work at the Half Moon Hotel right after."

We spent the night talking about Papa. She told me that between Benny and me, they had miscarried two babies. To understand why this kept happening, my father bought *Scientific American* magazines, and at night, when they came home from work, they read them aloud to each other. The key to my past turned in my brain when she told me that. The science book my father gave me, the direction he wanted for me.

Marm did not mention the notes from Mr. Soper, which had been so precious to me and sat like white boats on the table. Though they were simple office notes, to me they seemed like old letters from a long-lost love. Marm and I went to sleep very late, and before I turned off the gas, I tucked the notes under my pillow, hoping Marm would not ask about them.

April 16, 1907

Early this morning, Marm shook me awake from a dark dream of jungles and machetes, soldiers marching along a beach, my father with his eyes closed, finally at peace.

She started the stove fire and put the porridge water to boil. I glanced at her face in the pink dawn coming through the window; she seemed younger somehow, lighter. More whole. I wondered if she, too, had dreamt of Papa. Last night she told me things about him I never knew—her stories filled a place in me, that hollow space where he had been.

She stood by the window for long minutes without speaking, until the water boiled. I wondered what she was thinking. She served me a bowl of oatmeal and stood over me, looking down at me.

"I haven't had a chance to talk with you about the court case, Prudence," she said.

I picked up my spoon, feeling my skin more sensitive suddenly. She saw that I had put the notes away, Mr. Soper's notes to me.

A small, rusty door opened inside me, and I promised myself—no more secrets.

"I may have made a terrible mistake," I said.

She nodded knowingly. "Tell me," she said.

Keeping my eyes on the table, I told her of the spying and bribing in the case of Mary Mallon. I spoke about the morning with Jonathan, and how Mr. Soper saved me. I confessed my love for my chief. It all came spilling out, and I could not stop myself. I didn't want to stop. I had needed to tell her for months about these things, and now, finally, I did.

When I finished, she walked to the sink, where she stood with her back to me without saying a word. I waited for her to speak, frightened of what she might say. I could think of no defense for myself.

In a low voice, she said, "You work from eight in the morning until six at night with Mr. Soper."

She turned then, and said, "That is a lot of time to spend with one's chief."

I nodded, terrified she would take the job away from me.

She continued, "On the weekend, I'd expect you'd want to go out with your young friends, perhaps find a boy your age with whom you can visit the flickers, or the theater, or the nickelodeon."

"I study on the weekend," I said quietly.

"Prudence, each and every weekend you sit at that window and spend hours writing. You write in the evenings, and you never go out, unless it's with me. Why, since Anushka left, you haven't made a single friend. You spend all your time alone reading books, or writing letters, or scribbling in your tablets. Where is your life?"

I sensed my mouth dropping open—I thought of Anushka, who had not written a letter to me in weeks. I thought of the books Dr. Baker gave to me, and how I spent all my time studying them. I thought of my tablets, ten of which I had written so far.

And I thought, *She's right*.

Marm shook her head slowly and said, "I'm guilty of the same, since your father left. We have sealed ourselves up in this tomb—I still have your father's clothes in the closet, for goodness' sake! We have wanted to be with people who are dead or gone or simply not eligible—Mr. Charles Silver has been trying to tell me this for months, and I see it in you, too, Prudence. We must open our eyes and our hearts to people who are near and appropriate, flesh-and-blood humans who can return our affection in a proper manner."

Her words flew through me like arrows, the rightness of them landing straight inside my heart. I thought of my evenings and weekends, and I felt as if I'd been looking down, or in, for years. As if I were always telling myself a story, instead of living the story of my life. Suddenly Marm's words lifted my head, and I saw a bright, sunny sky with swarms of beautiful birds flying high, their colorful wings shining.

We have spent long years hiding ourselves, waiting for a man who will never come.

April 21, 1907

I tried it today. Instead of spending Sunday morning by the window with my tablet, I went out. I walked straight across town to the Hudson River, along the way admiring the crocuses and daffodils that shot up from the parks and lawns, and the pink blossoms on the trees, and the songs of the sparrows and chickadees, and the barks of the dogs, and the cries of the children. I admired the rainbow on the neck of a pigeon. At the river's edge, I watched wild boys swimming in the chilly water, and talked to a girl on the dock, a girl around my age with no ribbons on her collar. She seems thoughtful and kind, and her name is Betty.

Later in the afternoon, I met Dr. Baker at her home near Washington Square, a small and elegant set of rooms where she showed me her models of the human digestive system. We ate apple tarts and drank tea like two ladies while we talked about the function of the large intestine. She brought out her notes from the time she was in medical school, which greatly inspired me. Her careful drawings seemed familiar, and her attentive observations of the human organism were quite astute. She encouraged me to continue writing my tablets—not to the exclusion of all else, but rather as a supplement to my studies.

All day I found myself thinking of how I might translate what was happening into notes. Then I had to stop, to allow myself to live, as Marm said. I felt like a seesaw, tumbling down into thoughts, then working hard to pull back out again. Out into the sunlight, the fresh air, the voices of people and the sounds of moving traffic. After talking to Dr. Baker, I see what I must strive for. To keep the seesaw moving evenly from the inner world to the outer without becoming stuck in either.

Narcissus Sylvéstris

April 24, 1907

A great relief: Mary Mallon's case concluded today with the judge's decision. For the last few days, the families have been describing how they fell ill with the typhoid fever just weeks after hiring her. The weight of the evidence was too heavy to bear, it seems, and finally the judge stopped the proceedings.

He hammered his gavel to signal a break and looked at us from under his thick eyebrows.

"This case is very clear to me," he said. "I have read all the medical evidence submitted, and listened to enough testimony to see the pattern. Where Mary Mallon cooks, people are infected with the fever."

I could see Mary's head drop; my heart went out to her, for her terrible fate.

The judge went on, "I feel it's in the best interest of the

public to keep Mary Mallon on North Brother Island, where she will stay until medical science can find a solution to this problem. I order her returned to quarantine."

Voices cried out in the courtroom; Mary and O'Neal started to protest the judge's ruling, and the rummy huffed and fussed, half rising from his bench. Our lawyers patted each other's backs. Dr. Baker reached over and squeezed my shoulder. Mr. Soper held out his hand; I met his warm palm with mine and gave him a firm shake. I didn't have to look at him to know the immense relief he felt.

The judge hammered his gavel until the room quieted.

"It's not a question of innocence or guilt," the judge said, "but a matter of circumstance. Miss Mallon, the doctors on the island will try to make your life as comfortable as possible while they attempt to discover a cure for you. In the meantime, I cannot in good conscience free you. I'm sorry, but that is my decision."

He ordered the bailiff to take Mary away. The efficient man went to Mary and held her elbow; it seemed as if he had to physically lift her from the chair. As he led her past me, she turned her head and met my eyes. Her stare took my breath away, her anguish, her fury, like a caged creature, helplessness flooding her face red, like in my nightmare about her.

That nightmare.

The bailiff pulled her away. Over the movement around me, I watched her back as she crossed the room.

In the dream, Mary had pleaded with me.

A strange feeling came over me, a calmness, as if I felt my papa beside me. Mary had helped me to find him.

In my mind, I thanked her. I thanked her for being so stubborn, for without her obstinacy, I would never have known about Papa.

I wanted to help her in kind.

All I could give her was a promise.

I closed my eyes and made this silent vow: *Mary Mallon, if I get into medical school, I will go into the field of research. I'll do my best to discover why you carry typhoid, even though you are healthy.*

As I write it out now, I extend my promise: For Papa, for Benny, for all the girls and babies who've died in childbirth, I'll research the body—how it works, what sickens us, how to prevent those deaths that come too early.

I'll find answers to the questions that have haunted me for years.

Author's Note

When I was growing up, Typhoid Mary was an urban legend—
she had purposefully killed hundreds of people; she was an
evil murderess who spread disease to those she hated; she
was a comic-book villain. Her nickname had become part
of our lingo, a term for someone who carries a dangerous
disease and spreads it because they refuse to take proper
precautions. She was a symbol, not a person.

Clearly, I didn't know her real story.

When I met Mary Mallon in my research, her actual life
surprised me. A poor Irish immigrant, she tried to fit in with
wealthy New York families. She wanted a better life for herself and couldn't understand why she was being persecuted. I
saw how the deaths she caused were based on ignorance, not
willful intent to kill. She was a woman of her time—when
"bleeding," or opening up arteries to let out bad blood, was

still a regular practice among doctors, and the idea of bacteria, good or bad, had not yet become common knowledge. I felt I needed to tell Mary's true story, to restore her honor, in a way.

To me, Mary's life was a special kind of immigrant's tale, and I wanted to find a sympathetic protagonist who might understand her. It was my grandmother who allowed me to comprehend the immigrants' (and their children's) journey from "foreigner" to "American." I have a photo of Grandma as a girl slouching in front of a ride in Coney Island with a rebel look in her eye, wearing dark lipstick and a loose dress, probably taken around 1920. I knew that she fought against her own Eastern European father's Orthodox religious practice (a picture of him, a long-bearded rabbi, hung in her living room, but she never spoke about him). As a second-generation American Jew, Grandma's behavior conflicted with the stereotypes I often read about immigrant families who passed down their Old Country ways and stayed the same. Grandma couldn't have been more different from that stereotype. For instance, she held Passover every year, but lit no Shabbat candles, said no prayers, and rarely stepped foot inside a temple. By the time I met her, she was a tough old New Yorker, an American through and through.

In *You Must Remember This: An Oral History of Manhattan from the 1890s to World War II* and other books, I read the stories of those immigrants who fiercely wanted to be American, first and foremost, and did everything they could to become so. They told how they quickly modified their foreign habits by learning English, dressing in factory-made clothes, and going to the popular entertainments of the time. Many of them kept ties to their roots and religions but loosened the hold their past had on them. Mostly, what stayed the same was their cooking (which explains my grandmother's sumptuous Passover spread!).

I was influenced by my paternal grandmother as well. An independent woman, she raised my father alone while working full-time as a nurse. She was, in fact, the first nurse to use the X-ray machine. I will always remember the white hat, dress, and shoes that defined her.

Making fiction from reality is a tricky business. When piecing together the past from documents that may or may not be accurate, a writer has to arrive at her own interpretation of history. Jacob Riis's newspaper reports, books, and photographs helped me see how people really lived in the tenements. Despite their exaggerations, the yellow journalism of the day gave me a sense of the public's reactions to

Mary. Mr. Soper's own articles in medical journals showed me his path to Mary. Judith Walzer Leavitt's book *Typhoid Mary* explained why Mary herself didn't accept her label as a healthy carrier of typhoid fever.

I had to fill many gaps and accept the fact that the real players were going to have to engage with fictional characters. Mr. Soper, Dr. Baker, Mr. Briggs (or Biggs), Mr. Thompson, and of course Mary Mallon all existed, though their roles were altered to fit this story. The way Mr. Soper discovered Mary, through his investigations of the household, his interviews of the families, and ultimately the peach ice cream, is true. Mary's physical threats to Mr. Soper were real (though I think her verbal assaults were probably much worse!). The time line of events was the most difficult for me to re-create. I had to shorten the action of things. What took days or weeks in my book often really took months or years. It took Mr. Soper longer to find Mary. And she didn't petition the courts until 1909, years after she was captured.

I end my story with Mary's return to quarantine, leaving the reader to wonder what became of her. One year after her hearing, in 1910, a newly elected judge who wanted to maintain voter approval discharged Mary from North Brother Island. She returned to Manhattan, promising she would find other work and never cook for the public again. Just five years later, in 1915, a typhoid epidemic broke out at the Sloane Maternity Hospital. A cook named Mrs. Brown was discovered working in the kitchen. This cook had passed the typhoid bacteria to twenty-seven victims, two of whom died. Upon further investigation, it was found that Mrs. Brown was actually Mary Mallon. She simply never understood how, being healthy as a horse, she could be responsible for passing the typhoid fever. Or maybe, without help from the Department of Health, she was unable to find other work.

After Mary Mallon's second capture, she was returned to North Brother Island, where she spent the rest of her life, nearly twenty-five years, in a small cabin with her dog. The doctors never removed her gallbladder. In her lifetime, they found no remedy for a healthy carrier of the typhoid fever.